SPARKS OF DESIRE

An MMF Triad Love Story

Morgan Beacham

PRIORITIES PUBLISHING

Dedication

This book is dedicated to
my husband, my firefighter, my hero.
Thank you for supporting me in my adventures.
I wouldn't be who I am today without you.

TRIGGER WARNINGS

This novel is intended for mature audiences age 18+ only.

This novel contains:

—MMF, MM, and FM open door, spicy intimate scenes.

—reference to the death of a pregnant woman and unborn baby caused by pancreatic cancer.

—emergency medical scenes and firefighters sustaining injuries on scene.

If any of these are sensitive subjects for you, you may not want to read this book. I wish you peace, health, and comfort.

~Morgan

Pronunciation and Ten Codes

Pronunciation of Last Names
A Shift

Patrick Burrell, Captain	buh•rel
Nicholas Papciak	PAP•cee•ack
Terrance Stathes	STĀ•thēz
Roderick Muller	muh•ler
Drew Makris	mah•KRĒS
Owen Callaghan	kal•uh•han

Pronunciation of Last Names
B Shift

Amalia (Lia) Wiershen, Captain	WĒR•shen
Alejandro (Alex) Delgado	del•GAH•dō
Levi Kounovsky	koo•NŎV•skē
Brock Schultz	shuhltz
DeAndre Montpetit	mŌhn•puh•tē
Zander Ralbovsky	rahl•bĂHv•skē

10 Codes and What They Mean

10-4	Acknowledgement
10-23	Arrived at scene
10-58	Direct traffic
10-72	Report progress of fire
10-76	En route

Prologue

Drew
Ten Years Ago

THE CRACKLING OF THE loudspeaker fills the air, causing a jolt of anticipation to surge through me as Captain's voice buzzes on. The words she says change my life forever.

"Firefighter Makris, you have a personal emergency call on line 4."

My heart races as I rush to the phone thinking about my gorgeous pregnant wife at home, and pick up the receiver. "Firefighter Makris."

"Mr. Makris? My name is William. I'm a nurse at Henry Bassett Medical Center. Your wife has gone into labor and you need to get here right away. She's stable for now, but she's asking for you."

The words hang in the air, a mixture of hope and urgency. I hang up the phone, my mind focused on one thing - reaching Corinne at the hospital. I drive faster than I should and make it to the hospital in record time. Anyone would speed to get to the love of their life in the hospital having their first-born child, but I'm in a hurry for an additional reason. My wife, Corinne Makris, has pancreatic cancer. We found out when she was only two months pregnant and have been taking precautions every step of the way to ensure a healthy pregnancy and childbirth for her and Michael, our son.

Cori has been resilient and strong during this pregnancy, and she amazes me each and every day. She's followed all the doctors' and nurses' orders to a T and, relatively speaking, things have gone alright over the past six months. It hasn't been easy. Cori's been sick and had some terrible moments. The morning sickness from the pregnancy double-teamed her with nausea and fatigue from the cancer. Not only did Cori have to persevere while her body created a child, but she also endured abdominal pain, digestive problems, and so many trips to Burroughs Medical Center for treatments, it's become our second home. Now Michael is coming a month earlier than we expected, so my brain is befuddled with what-ifs and whys.

Tires screech as I swing into the parking lot, not caring whether I get a ticket. I have to get to my wife and son.

Running through the automatic doors at the entrance, I shout to the nearest nurse, "Makris. Wife is in labor! Where?"

They direct me to her room and I struggle for air as I enter to find tears streaming down her face and her shaking hands reaching out to me. I grab her hands, kiss them, and wipe her tears away, reassuring her that I'm here and I'm not going anywhere.

"Thank God you're here, Drew. I couldn't do this without you. Dr. Mayer says Michael is coming today. I know we were trying to make it to the nine-month mark, but my water broke. I called 911 and the ambulance just arrived, so I haven't been here long."

Brushing her brown bangs off her forehead, I apologize because it's the only thing I know to do right now. "I'm so sorry I wasn't home. I hated going to work knowing you might need me. What else has the doctor said?" I need to stay calm, for Cori's sake. I need to get the information and assess the situation.

"Dr. Mayer said that she thinks it won't be long. With the complication of the cancer, they'll have to do a cesarean section. They're getting the operating room prepped now. Drew, what if..." she trails off with a sob.

"Shhhh...Baby." I kiss her forehead. "All we can do is take things one step at a time. We'll try to relax until it's time for surgery. It looks like the nurses are taking great care of you. They know about the pancreatic cancer and they're taking extra precautionary measures to make sure everything will be alright."

I can't let her think this way. I need to get her mind on something else that will distract her from worrying so she can relax. I squeeze her hand and encourage her, saying, "We can do this. We can get through this. We're one hell of a team, you and me. We've gotten this far. Soon, we'll be able to hold our son in that comfortable rocking chair you got for Michael's nursery. You're making me one happy Daddy."

"What if things don't go well in surgery? You know there are so many complications and we need to be prepared for anything. You know where my will is and you remember that we agreed my sister would be Michael's godmother if anything happens to me, right?" She has a tormented look on her beautiful face.

"Don't talk like that, Babe. Yes, we've got everything ready for every situation that could possibly happen. We need to relax and pray that everything will be fine. I'll take care of you and Michael. I'll do whatever I have to do to make sure you're both healthy. We've got some of the best doctors and nurses in all of Illinois here helping us. Now, how about we do some of those Lamaze breathing techniques?" As soon as we inhale, Dr. Mayer walks in.

"I'm sorry, but it's time. Corinne, we need to take you back to surgery. Mr. Makris, you can wait here and the nurses will keep you informed with constant updates." She stands holding her hands in front of her, trying to look calm and confident in the face of an intimidating surgery.

I hug Cori as tightly as I can without hurting her. "Babe, I love you. You are strong. I'll be waiting for you when you get done."

Pressing her forehead against mine, she takes my face in her gentle hands, saying, "I love you. Thank you, Drew, for being the best husband and father to Michael and me. You make me complete. Michael and I will see you soon." Cori brushes her lips against mine before they wheel her out of the room to the surgical ward.

Watching the nurses push Cori through the double doors, I collapse onto the chair in her hospital room. My head hangs in my hands as I try to support myself physically while I'm being obliterated mentally. The two most important people of my life just went through those doors and I don't know if or when I'll see them again.

I met and fell in love with Corinne almost immediately. She is perfect for me and she's going to be an incredible mother. We planned everything we could once we decided to have a child. We read all the books. Listened to the doctors. Took the Lamaze and birthing classes together. Then, two months after finding out Cori was pregnant and we would be parents, we got the news that she had pancreatic cancer.

Cancer. I've never hated anything more in my life. Even though we knew cancer is one of the leading causes of deaths, we still spoke with all the doctors about the pregnancy to weigh our options. Corinne is young. The doctors said that was a huge blessing because pancreatic cancer usually occurs in people who are older. People have been known to overcome pancreatic cancer; to live a comparatively normal life. We hoped and prayed that we could beat this monster and have our happy little family of three. We knew this would be our only child because of the cancer, so Michael would be that much more special to us. Every moment with my wife and child would be such a treasure to me.

***

JUST AS I'M IMAGINING pushing Michael on a swing while Cori sits nearby on a picnic blanket, the doctor comes out of the double doors. *I can't read her face. What happened? What is she thinking?* She sits in the chair beside me and her tired eyes meet mine.

"Mr. Makris, your wife fought a tough battle, but I'm sorry to inform you that she and your baby did not make it through surgery. Once we began, we encountered a large tumor which had taken over Corinne's liver. We also discovered the radiation and chemotherapy treatments had some negative impacts on your baby, which we knew was a risk. I'm so sorry for your loss. Is there anyone we can call to be with you?" The words echo like I'm trudging through a tunnel into increasing darkness.

All the oxygen has been sucked from my lungs. My heartbeat has gone silent and words escape me. Dr. Mayer waits for my answer, but there is none. I just shake my head. There isn't anyone to call that can help me. I'll contact Corinne's parents and sister, but they live in Arizona, so they can't be here anytime soon to help. My parents passed when I was a teenager. There is no one. I'm alone now.

I pull out of the hospital parking lot with zero fortitude to do anything or go anywhere. I brake at the stoplight and glance in the rearview mirror at the car seat we never got to use. How will I find a way to continue on without Cori and our baby?

CHAPTER 1

Emerson

I STILL GET THAT giddy feeling when I hear the familiar rumble of my husband's truck pulling into the driveway after a long stretch at work. Most of the time, I feel like the luckiest woman alive. I married my high school sweetheart and we have a loving, meaningful marriage. We have three intelligent, caring children. We both have our dream jobs and, although we're not rich, I'd say we live comfortably. I can't help but think... *What more could anyone ask for?*

Owen turns off the engine and heads inside. At the door, I reach up on my tiptoes to greet his wide shoulders with open arms, relishing the comfort of my firefighter's bear hug and the feeling of his familiar kiss. I'm so glad he's home because life has been crazy without him here.

Murphy's Law prevailed over the last three days. If it could go wrong, it did. Owen got stuck on mandatory overtime on the same day I needed him to go to Keegan's parent teacher conference, so I had to reschedule it for after I got off work and handle it alone. Declan had a huge meltdown when his hamster died. The cat puked on the living room carpet. I could go on and on, but he's home now, so I tell myself to focus on the positive.

"How was your shift?" I can feel his weariness, the tension in his muscles, as he wraps his tattooed arms around me. He smells like diesel fuel, grease, smoke, and fire—the natural, blended aroma of the Riverfront Fire Department.

His response comes in a tired voice filled with frustration. Owen drops his bag, hangs up his coat, and kicks his shoes off while answering. "It was a shit show. They held ten guys on overtime today because we're so short on staff. The only reason I didn't have to work is because I've already been there for three days. I'm home today, but I have to work overtime tomorrow. I'll be at the station for three days straight...again."

His somber brown eyes look as though it pains him to tell me this. I'm used to it. This is the life of a firefighter and his family. This is how things have been for a while now. Even though it wears on me, too, I do my best to be supportive.

"It's okay, Honey. We'll enjoy today together, have dinner with the kids when they get home from school, and we'll get through this. One day at a time. Hopefully, your management will get smart soon and hire more people. We signed on for 48 hour shifts, not 72 hours, and that time already includes built in overtime. They can't keep doing this to you guys. Everyone will burn out sooner or later. Let's get you some breakfast and you can tell me why it was such a shit show." That's how he describes almost every shift he works every time we have this conversation.

I pour Owen a glass of juice while he pops a sausage biscuit in the microwave for breakfast. On a normal Wednesday morning, I would have already left for work with Declan in tow before Owen even got home from work, but Winter Break started today, so the kids and I are out of school for two weeks.

Sitting down at the table with his breakfast, he continues. "On top of only getting one day off this week, I have so much to do that I can't even relax on my day off. There's no time. It would help if they'd hire some people, host a fire academy, and get some more people on the floor. Papciak is out with a torn ligament in his knee. Not his fault, but that increases the OT."

"Papciak? You mean Nick? You confuse me with all the nicknames and last names. I know I'm a teacher, but doing roll call for the guys at the station is crazy." They're all like brothers, though, so I do my best to keep up with all the names. I sit down at the table to keep him company while he eats.

"Yeah, Nick. He hurt his knee in a brush fire we had not too long ago. Won't be back on the floor for a few more weeks. All the guys are exhausted, but I'm kind of worried about Makris. He's always at the station, working overtime for other people."

"Aw, why is Drew offering to work other people's overtime? I know he wants to help, but he needs time off, too." Drew is one of the guys I do know well. He and Owen have become best friends ever since Drew moved here from Illinois three years ago. He's the handsome firefighter that comes over quite often. I've also seen him at station events, ceremonies, and retirement parties. He's always been kind to me and the kids, and he and Owen have become inseparable. If they're not on shift together, they're helping each other out or hanging out fishing.

"Whenever someone doesn't want their OT, he'll work it for them so they can go home. I know it's because he doesn't have a family to go home to; it's just him. He even told me last shift that he let his apartment go and moved his stuff to storage."

"What? Why?! He has to have a place to go when he's not working. He can't work his life away. I feel so bad for him. He must be lonely."

"He says if there's no one there to go home to, why go home? Drew left Illinois and moved out here to Virginia to take a job with our fire station. He got an apartment in the city, but he was barely ever there. Won't even get a dog or a cat. He said he hated it in the city, so when his lease agreement was up, he just decided not to renew. He pays a small storage fee and just stays at the station whenever he can. Banks away his money. He's a volunteer firefighter, too, so if he's not working, he's at that station or at a buddy's house."

"Why don't you invite him to come over again next time both of you are off? It'll give him a chance to get out of the station. A change of scenery and a home-cooked meal will do him some good. It'd be nice for us to do something different for a change, too. We can have a board game day or you guys can fish off the dock." He nods like it's no big deal, but I can tell he's worried about Drew.

"He wouldn't want you to go through the trouble of cooking just for him. He knows how busy you are and he hates being the center of attention." Owen is right. I remember at the last retirement ceremony, Drew just hung out in the back where there was standing room only.

"Alright. Invite the guys from the station and their families to come over on Sunday at noon. I'll invite Lauren and her husband over, too. She's been telling me she wants to hang out, anyway. We'll put the game on and have some good food."

"That sounds good." Owen steps over to my side of the kitchen table, pulls me up by my hand, and envelops me in one of his enormous hugs that I love so much. *If only we could take it a step further.* The kids are here and there are things to do. *Maybe tonight.*

Owen kisses me on the cheek before walking to the back door. "I'll be outside if you need me. I have tons to do."

Just as he leaves, Keegan comes out of her room with her phone to her ear, saying, "Mom, is it okay if Melanie stays the night tonight?"

"I don't know, Keegan. It's the first day of Winter Break. I'd like some peace and quiet so I can relax. I'm around students all day, every day. Plus, last time she stayed, you didn't do your chores like you were supposed to and you two were up all night long."

"I promise I'll do my chores and we'll be quiet so we don't keep you up. You won't even know she's here," Keegan says.

"Alright, fine. If you don't do your chores and help around the house, then she's not coming over again for a month."

Keegan squeals into her phone, telling Melanie that I said yes, and runs off down the hallway, back to her room. I head that way, too, to check on Declan in his play room.

He's playing Minecraft on the TV and there's a YouTube video playing on his iPad.

"Hey Declan, how are things going in here?" I sit down next to him on the old couch we've had since before Keegan was born. He's focused on his game and doesn't respond right away, so I clear my throat and say, "Earth to Declan?"

Never taking his eyes off the screen, he mumbles, "Hey, Mom. When did you get here?"

"Declan, you really need to do something else besides sit and play video games all the time. You're not spending your entire break from school in here all alone. I asked you how you are doing."

"I'm good. I'm building a house in the Nether, which Preston says is the safest place in the world. I'm building it with purpur blocks, just like he did! Isn't that cool?"

"What are purpur blocks? Where is Nether? I've never heard of it before. Is Preston a friend from school?" Sometimes it's like he speaks another language.

His eyebrows almost shoot off the top of his forehead. "Mooooom, Preston? From PrestonPlayz? Don't you remember him?" He asks with an edge of annoyance.

"Ah, yes, that YouTuber you like to watch. Of course. How could I forget? I'll leave you to it, but you have about an hour to play and then I expect you to do your chores, which you didn't do yesterday, and get outside for some fresh air." All I can do is shake my head.

"Fiiiiiine. Is Dad home today?" He asks as I'm walking through the door.

"Yes, but he's only home today. He has to go back to work tomorrow." I hate having to tell the kids Owen won't be here for his scheduled two days off. They see him as rarely as I do.

"Aw, maaaaan. Why's he always gotta work? He was supposed to help me practice soccer."

"There's a lot of overtime right now, bud. They're short-staffed and he doesn't have a choice. I can help you practice soccer if you want. We'll have plenty of time over break." He just shakes his head and groans, as usual. He's getting to that age where groaning and mumbling are the only languages he speaks.

Owen's working outside. Grady, our oldest son, is at work today at the shipyard. Keegan and Declan clearly have their own agendas for today. Guess I'll get started on my to do list since everyone else is busy.

CHAPTER 2

Owen

WE WENT ABOUT OUR day as we usually do, taking care of chores around the house that don't get done when we're at work. Unfortunately, we didn't get much more time together today. I love what I do for a living, but it takes me away from my family so much that I worry about them. Emerson is strong, but I hate that my job makes her have to be so strong all the time.

I made barbeque chicken tonight for dinner, so after we ate, I went outside to clean up the grill. With that done, we all sat and watched the news in the living room for a while. After getting my ass kicked at Wheel of Fortune and Jeopardy, the kids head off to their bedrooms for the night. As Emerson washes the dishes in the sink, I just look at her and think to myself how lucky I am to have her. Not many women would put up with the shit my job throws at us.

"I missed you," I whisper in Emerson's ear as I walk up behind her. She dries her hands on a towel as I wrap my arms around her waist and run my nose along her neck, taking in her delicious scent. She spins around in my arms and puts her hands on my chest.

"Oh, you did, huh? I couldn't tell since you were outside all day long. Even though we were both home today, I still didn't get to see you."

I pick her up and set her on the counter next to the sink. She wraps her arms around my neck, squeezing her legs around my waist. I work out every day I'm at the station, so picking up her voluptuous body requires little effort on my part. I love to have her in my arms and wrapped around me.

"I know, Emerson. There's just so much to do. You can always come outside to hang out with me if you want." I leave little kisses along her jawline and down her neck.

"I would, but you know I have things I have to catch up on, too."

"I know, and I appreciate everything you do around here to make things work with my awful schedule lately. I want to show you how much I missed you since the kids are in bed." We're both tired, but it's not often we get a chance to be alone, so I'm going to take advantage of it while I can.

I carry her from the kitchen to our bedroom, still kissing her the whole way. Her little moans are turning me on and I'm sure she can feel me growing between her legs as I lay her down on the bed, still hovering over her. I slide my hands down over her body and when I move them back up, I slip them under her shirt and caress her smooth skin.

"I always miss you when you're at work, but I love making up for it when you come home," she tells me as she pulls my head down to kiss me. She slides her tongue between my lips, and I continue my perusal of every inch of her skin while we enjoy a slow kiss. After taking off her shirt and expertly unhooking her bra, my mouth devours her nipples, sucking and licking her breasts like they're the most delicious meal I've ever had while she traces the muscles in my arms like she's memorizing them.

Emerson sits up, pushing me to a standing position, and pulls off my shirt. She leaves sensual kisses all over my chest and stomach while unbuckling my belt and then my jeans to push them and my boxers down to the floor. She kneels in front of me and all I can think is *I don't deserve this gorgeous woman*. My dick is hard and I can't wait to feel her warm mouth around it. She grabs onto my thighs like she needs something to hold on to, licks her lips, and slides them down my shaft, drawing a low growl from my throat. I soak up the sight of her on her knees, looking up at me with those beautiful blue eyes while she sucks on me. My fingers slide through her long, brown hair, and I tighten my hands a little, pulling just enough to tell her she's mine without hurting her...too much.

She licks and sucks me like she's savoring me, tasting every bit of skin she can get to, then she sucks my dick back into her mouth until I feel the back of her throat. Emerson wraps her fingers around the base of me that won't fit in her mouth and massages me with her hand. Feeling her swallow me into her throat drives me wild, and I have to pull her head away. Through gritted teeth, I tell her, "Emerson, it's been a while. You're going to make me come, and I'd rather be inside of you than in your mouth."

I take her hands and pull her up, kicking off my pants, and I claim her mouth with mine.

In between kisses, she says, "If we did this more often, maybe you'd last longer." *Wiseass*. I spin her around so she's leaning forward on the bed, and then tug her pants and panties off, so now she stands bare naked with her ass pushed out toward me.

"That's better," I grumble. "God, what a gorgeous ass." I grab her hips and line myself up with her opening, firmly pushing in until I'm stretching her and I'm as deep as I can go. Without time to adjust to me, she gasps unexpectedly, and I tell her, "That's what you get for being a smartass."

"I'll definitely have to stop being a smartass, then, huh?" She says playfully.

"Emerson, you feel so good squeezing my dick," I whisper in her ear. I'm so glad she has an IUD so we don't have to use a condom. "I love the feeling of being inside you," I rumble, which elicits a sexy moan from her that makes me even harder. I pull almost all the way out, then push back in and find a steady rhythm that I've been craving for the past three days while I've been at work. The heat in the bedroom is stifling, and it feels like we're in the desert, but I don't care. I need this woman.

"Owen, I'm not going to last much longer." She says as I pound into her from behind.

"Thank God, Emerson, because I can't hold on any longer," I tell her. I let go, releasing a shitload of pent up frustration, and come inside of my girl. She's right there with me, spasming around me, clinging to the bedspread for traction. When we come down from that euphoric feeling, I wrap my arms around her waist, stand her up against my chest, and drop light kisses on her neck. She heads into the bathroom to clean up and I flop down on the bed. When she comes back out, my eyes are halfway closed, and she snuggles in beside me as I wrap her in my arms.

I am so lucky to have this woman in my life. She's right. I wish we could do this more often. Sometimes we're lucky and get some time together in the morning when I get home, but usually life gets so hectic that we're exhausted by the time we go to bed and we crash without having any quality time together. As much as I'm enjoying this snuggle time, I can barely keep my eyes open.

"Owen?" she whispers.

"Yeah, Babe?"

"Thanks for not falling asleep on me tonight." I can feel her smiling in the dark.

"Sure thing," I tell her, smacking her ass. "You can pay me back by not snoring tonight."

Emerson

I hear Owen whisper in the darkness, "Bye, Babe. I love you. I'll see you Sunday morning." He kisses my lips and then I'm alone again. I drift in and out of sleep until the sun comes up and I finally crawl out of bed.

I feel like I'm constantly in my classroom during the week, so cleaning and laundry gets done on my days off. Some days, I'm in my classroom until six or seven o'clock at night even though school gets out at 3:45. Winter break is my time to play catch up on big chores like cleaning the oven and cleaning the carpets in the house. I also try to catch up on grading from the last few weeks and get ahead of the game for January, which can be a tough month for teachers and students.

When Owen is only home one or two days a week from the station, his To Do list adds up, too. I know he has a million things to take care of and I probably don't even know what half of them are. I don't know what I'd do if I didn't have him. On days like yesterday where he's home but we still barely see each other because he's working outside and I'm working inside, I really wish he had a regular nine-to-five job where he worked forty hours each week and was home every night. Being able to see him every night and all day on two full days off would be a significant change from his current schedule and would make such a dramatic difference in our lives. The kids would get more time with their dad and I imagine life would be much easier. Throw in not having to worry about the potential danger of his career and it sounds perfect to me.

With all the extra overtime the guys are working right now, they end up working about 120 to 144 hours each week. It's hard to keep a relationship healthy when you're barely ever together. He loves his job, though. I'd never ask him to leave it. He was a firefighter when I met him. I couldn't ask him to change that part of him.

My phone rings and I set the laundry basket down to answer it.

"Hey Lauren! How's your Winter Break going so far?"

"Ugh, it's okay, I guess. I might as well be at work. Lamont couldn't care less that I'm home. What have you been up to?"

"Catching up on things around the house...cleaning, laundry, you know, the stuff we don't get to do because we're working all the time. What are you doing?"

"Same thing. I wanted to go out to lunch today, but when I mentioned it to Lamont, he said he doesn't have time. He gets an hour lunch break every day. I don't know why he can't meet me for lunch somewhere."

"Maybe he's really busy at work?"

"He's always really busy at work. He needs to eat lunch, though, right? I figure it's a little bit of time we can spend together while I'm on break from work."

"Yeah, that would be nice for you guys to spend some time together, even if it's just half an hour."

"Most days, when he gets home from work around 6:00pm, he'll eat dinner, then he has to leave again. I guess I can't complain. At least he comes home to sleep eventually every night. I know you miss Owen when he's at work."

"I do, but it'll get better when they hire some more people and there's less overtime. He was home yesterday, but he left this morning at 6:00am for another three days."

"Damn, girl. I don't know how you do it. Y'all got plans for the break? Doing anything fun?"

"I'd like to, but it'd have to be just me and the kids. We'll find something fun to do. Hey, we're going to have a cookout and watch the game on Sunday. You and Lamont want to come? Bring the kids, too."

"Yes. I'd love to get out of the house. I'll try to talk Lamont into coming with us. What can I bring?"

"Oooh, bring those nachos you made last time we got together. They were delicious."

"You got it. See you Sunday."

CHAPTER 3

Drew

FRIDAY NIGHT: THE BEST night of the week, according to some bachelors. Not me. Papciak set me up with a blind date that I was adamantly opposed to, but I finally gave in because, hell, it's been six months since I've been out with a woman and he wouldn't leave me alone about it. He swears this woman is spectacular in every way. She's a friend of his girlfriend, but I'm not sure he's ever met her.

I guess? She sounds as excited about our date as I am.

Pulling up to her house at 6:55pm, I park in the driveway between two huge brick pillars, straighten the collar on my polo shirt, and tread up the sidewalk to her doorstep.

When I press the doorbell, I can hear the fancy chime inside, but the door stays closed. I'm sure she heard the doorbell. Unless, maybe I've got the wrong house?

I check the address plaque and press the doorbell again. I hear the chimes again. They pretty much play an entire two-minute symphony.

A man in his sixties finally opens the door. *Wasn't expecting him.*

"Hi, I'm Drew. I'm here to pick up Cecilia. Is she ready?"

Without a word to me, he turns his head and beckons, "Cecilia, darling, there's a gentle... a man at the door for you."

We're off to a great start.

Cecilia comes down the elaborate stairs behind him in a red, floor-length ball gown with a slit up to her hip, still putting on diamond earrings that are five inches long.

"Finally, you're here." *Finally? You're still getting ready.* "Father, fasten my bracelet."

She turns to the man, and he does what she tells him, saying, "You look stunning, Sweetheart." He helps her put on her fur cover up. *Is that made of real...anything?*

"Thanks bunches. Love you! Don't wait up!" Her heels click clack on the floor as she shuts the door.

"Hi. You must be Drew."

"Hi, Cecilia. It's so good to meet you. You look nice tonight."

"Of course, I do." *Wow.* "Where are you taking me?"

"I'd like to take you to one of my favorite restaurants. It overlooks the river and even from an inside table on this chilly night, we'll have a beautiful view. They have delicious food."

"Ugh, damn. I was hoping you'd take me to La Chateau de Gens Pretentieux," she whines.

"Maybe we can plan on that for a later date," I tell her. We walk to the truck and when I open the door, she looks from the truck to me with wide eyes.

"How am I supposed to get up there?" *If you'd dressed casually, like I'd recommended, you'd have no problem.*

"Here," I say, clasping my fingers together in front of her at knee height for her to step on to help boost her up. "I'll help you up." She's skinny as a beanpole, so it's easy to lift her up. I usually prefer women with a little more to hold on to, though.

We clumsily get her in the truck and I shut the door. Hopping in, my favorite Toby Keith song comes on when

I start the engine and I tap along on the steering wheel. Cecilia reaches over to change the radio station.

I usually enjoy the peace and quiet as I drive, but as we navigate Highway 17, the various radio station buzz fills my ears as Cecilia skips through to find something she likes. Eventually, she just turns the radio off with a dramatic sigh.

"Nothing on the radio tonight?"

"No. I usually listen to satellite radio. I have all my favorite stations programmed in on my father's radio."

"Do you listen to satellite radio in your car, too?"

"I don't have a car. I don't drive. My father drives me anywhere I need to go in his Jaguar."

"Jagwires are nice. So, you live with your dad, then?"

"No, it's not Jagwire. It's Jag-war. And yes, I live with my dad, but only temporarily. I'll be moving out as soon as my agent finds a good fit for me."

"What do you do for a living?"

"Isn't it obvious?" she asks incredulously. "I'm a model."

"Oh, I can see that. You're certainly very pretty. What sort of things do you model?"

"Only the finest clothing, jewelry, and cosmetics."

"I've heard modeling can be a tough job. It takes a lot of dedication and perseverance. What was your last modeling job like?" *She seems to enjoy talking about her job.*

"It was about seven years ago and I worked for a large corporation that sold couture healing cream for all skin-care types. They held an ethereal world view of equity for all."

"What kind of healing cream was it? Maybe I should check it out."

"It was Vaseline, okay. Vaseline. They have some great lotions and cremes," she answers irritably. *Maybe I should let that one go. Seems like a touchy subject.*

"Do you have something in the works for your next job? Anything lined up?"

"My agent takes care of all of that. It'll probably be in Paris or Milan...somewhere like that."

"That's interesting," I say as she freshens up her makeup in the visor mirror. I figure maybe it's time to tell her a little about me.

"I'm a firefighter and EMT for our local fire station. It's absolutely my dream j..." I begin.

"My ex-boyfriend's sister's husband was a firefighter," she cuts me off. "He was such a jerk. Always working and never came home to take care of her."

"We do work long shifts. It's not an easy schedule for us or our loved ones," I chime in.

"He just never wanted to be home with her. Loved his job more than anything else. You know, about nine years ago, I did a modeling job with some firefighters. It was an ad for a jewelry company. They were hot. Cuter than you, not that you aren't cute or anything."

"Uh, thank you?" *I'm not sure how to take this woman. I need to try to find some common ground or tonight is going to be a disaster.*

I park in the restaurant's small gravel parking lot and walk around to open her door. Cecilia seems a little wobbly on her high heels in the gravel, so I offer her my hand, but she refuses it. Inside the front door, the hostess asks, "Table for two?"

"Yes, please," I reply. "I made a reservation for Makris. We'd love a river view by the window if you have one."

"I don't really care if we have a river view. I am not a nature person," Cecilia tells the hostess. *Duly noted.*

At the table, I pull out her chair for her, trying to turn on the charm any chance I get. We get settled and begin looking at our menus.

"Do they not have escargot here?" She says loud enough for everyone around us to hear.

"No, I don't think so. They have quite a few different types of food here; Greek, American, Italian. That's one reason I thought this might be a good place to eat tonight. They serve a little bit of everything...seafood, steaks, burgers."

"I don't really see anything I like. I guess I'll deal with having a Ceasar Salad. I don't want to go over my calorie limit, anyway. I need to make sure I'm fit for the next round of photography I endure. It is so exhausting. Sometimes I wish I could just have an easy job, like a teacher or something."

She must not know what teachers do for a living. My friend, Emerson, is continuously exhausted from her teaching job. I'm going to let that one go.

"Their salads are good here. I think you'll like it. I'm going to have the Fried Seafood Combo. Their shrimp is amazing."

When the server comes over, we order our meals and descend into silence. *I almost prefer the silence to her chatting. I really should try to make conversation again.* "What do you like to do for fun?"

"I like going to the spa for manicures and massages. It's important to practice self-care when you're in my line of work."

"That sounds relaxing. I've never had a professional massage before."

"I get one at least once a week. You should try it. It feels so good. It brings out your dolphins and eases pain." She sighs like she's getting a massage right now.

"Do you mean it releases endorphins?" I ask.

"Irregardless," she mumbles and takes a sip of her drink.

The server brings our meals right as Cecilia puts her drink down and I thank the Heavens above for the reprieve. We begin eating and spend some time enjoying our food. I enjoy the sunset over the river, even though Cecilia might not. The purples and blues are gorgeous and the twinkling lights over the bridge add a magical touch.

"So, let's get to know each other better. How old are you?" I ask her.

"I can't believe you would ask me that! What a faux pas!"

"I'm so sorry. I didn't mean to be rude. I was just wondering if we were close in age, that's all." *And wondering how old you have to be to move out of your dad's house...*

I give up. I'm not sure I can say anything right tonight.

We finish our meal with a one-sided conversation, during which Cecilia tells me about her new makeup line she's creating. I don't know much about makeup and it seems every time I say something, I offend her, so I just keep quiet and listen.

When she's finished eating and talking, I venture, "I had planned to go for a walk on the beach after dinner, but if you'd rather, we could go see a movie. I know you said you're not a fan of nature."

"Ya know, Drew, I think I'd like for you to just take me home. I don't think we're a good match. You barely spoke to me at all tonight. It's hard to have a conversation with someone when they won't communicate with me." Rather than feeling hurt, I'm relieved. I didn't really want to continue this night, but I wanted to be a gentleman and take her on a proper date, since that's what I promised.

"I understand. I'll take you home, then."

After I pay the bill, we tolerate a silent ride back to her house—her dad's house. As we approach her front door, I tell her, "It's been a nice evening. Thank you for spending time with me."

"Would you like to come in?" she asks. I couldn't be more shocked, for several reasons.

"Not tonight, thank you. Take care." I make my way back to my truck as quickly as possible before anything else goes wrong tonight.

On the ride home, I wonder to myself about relationships and life. I haven't dated much after I lost my wife and son, but when I do, I can't seem to find the right person for me. Are my standards too high? Am I expecting too much? I just want a down-to-earth woman who is easy to talk to, caring, and intelligent. Will I ever find anyone like that? Maybe it would be less complicated to simply embrace my solitude and stop dating altogether.

CHAPTER 4

Owen

WE SHOULD BE GETTING snow this late in December, but rain is coming down just enough to make it miserable and dreary outside; damn Virginia weather. It's a chilly 38 degrees and cloudy, which makes me glad we didn't plan this little shindig outside. Inviting some people over was an awesome idea on Emerson's part. It's nice to get out of our normal routine and do something different.

I made some kickass barbeque and coleslaw for sandwiches today and I've got a marinated brisket in the oven that smells like heaven. Emerson's playing her music, dancing in the kitchen while she cooks. She's diligently making her mouthwatering homemade potato salad, macaroni and cheese, mashed potatoes, green bean casserole, and tons of appetizers and desserts to snack on.

The football game is on TV and the kids are already playing Monopoly and Scrabble with the other kids that are here—some of their friends from the neighborhood and Burrell's daughter from his first marriage. Grady's at his girlfriend's house, of course. He's barely ever here anymore between her house and working full time. I'm proud of that guy. He's looking for an affordable apartment to rent. I hope he can find something decent in this insane real estate market we have right now.

A couple that lives two doors down, Lamont and Lauren, came over to hang out. Papciak, another firefighter from the Riverfront Fire Department, is here with his girlfriend, Cate, hanging out on the couch because of his busted knee. She seems uninterested in talking to anyone and is staring at her phone like it's a lifeline. Muller is here, but says he has to leave early. Didn't say why.

Captain Amalia Wiershen and most of the other guys at the station couldn't make it today because they're on shift. Burrell and Stathes are arm wrestling at the table. They're always fucking competing to see who's better. I'm still on the lookout for Drew as I stroll into the kitchen to see what I can help Emerson with.

"Could you take out the trash for me while there's a break in the rain? That way, everyone will be able to clean up after themselves and it'll be less work for us later." She winks at me. "Other than that, I've got things under control. Is everyone having a good time?"

As I start to gather the trash bag out of the can, I nod. "Seems like it. Smiles all around and no complaints. Well, except that the kids are getting hungry. As always. I think everyone's here who's coming, except for Drew. I haven't heard from him."

"He'll be here. You know you can count on him. Especially when there's food involved." She laughs.

I take the trash bag outside to throw it in the bed of my truck and see Drew pulling up to the house. He parks on the street and meanders up to me. "Hey, Callaghan. How's it going?"

"Good, Makris. Where you been? Everyone else is here. How are things?" I throw the trash bag in the truck bed with my left hand and shake his hand with my right.

"Yeah, sorry about that. I was hanging out at the volunteer station for a while and dozed off waiting for a call. Never did get one. Anyway, I'm here now," he says as he holds out his hand to feel misty rain drops starting to come down again. "Let's get inside before we get soaked."

Closing the front door, I introduce Drew to the people he doesn't know.

"Drew, this is Lamont and Lauren Washington. They live two doors down, and Lauren works with Emerson at Chesapeake Elementary School." They all shake hands and say hello as I motion toward Nick's girlfriend.

"This is Nick's girlfriend," I begin.

"My name is Coruscate, but you can call me Cate," she says, extending her hand to Drew. "Are you a firefighter?" He nods in answer and her eyes sparkle.

"Most of the guys here are firefighters," he says. "Just like Nick."

"That's so cool," Cate replies. "Have you been on any fire calls lately?"

Nick knows we're not into talking about the calls outside of work, so he takes her hand and says, "Cate, I can fill you in on the fire calls we've had lately. Let's go sit. My knee is starting to hurt."

"You haven't even been on any calls lately because you're on desk duty. And besides, you told me we were going to the station. How come we're here?" She gripes as they find a seat and Nick shakes his head.

Drew already knows the guys from the station, so he says his hellos to everyone and we make our way into the kitchen.

"Hey there, Emerson. How are you doing, Hun?" Drew asks.

She looks up from the chocolate chip cookies she's taking off the cookie sheet and smiles. "Hey Drew!" She scampers over to give him a hug. "I'm doing okay. I'm glad you're here! How've you been?"

Hugging her back, he says, "I'm doing fine. What can we help you with in here? Looks like you've been working all day. Everything smells delicious."

"Nothing right now. I've got it all under control, but Declan has been wanting to practice soccer if you guys aren't too old for it. Looks like those rain clouds have moved on."

"Too old?!" Drew and I say at the same time.

"Don't you worry, we got this," I tell her. "Declan! Bring that soccer ball out here, son," I shout to him down the hall.

"Anyone up for a game?" Declan inquires, bouncing the ball off his head.

Considering how competitive most of us are, all the guys are geared up to show how old we are *not*. We divvy ourselves into two teams and rambunctiously play a backyard game of soccer to help Declan practice his skills. Declan scores the most goals and outruns any firefighter on the field, of course. When the score is five to one and Stathes falls in the mud, we call it a game and everyone goes back in to watch TV.

Laughing, Emerson hands Stathes a towel so he can clean up in the bathroom while everyone makes their way to the living room. She looks at me and Drew and says, "Perfect timing, guys! Here, help me put these dishes on the table so we can eat." She hands each of us dishes to place on the table and we continue until everything is set out for all the guests. When we're done, she gives me a quick kiss and says, "Thank you both for helping. Will you please let everyone know they can come on in to eat now?"

I walk her backwards toward the counter and turn that quick kiss into a long one, sliding my tongue in to feel hers. Pressing my hips against hers, so she clearly knows how much I want her, I take her face in my hands and kiss the hell out of her. She tastes like the brownie batter I saw her sneak a lick of earlier before she put the spoon in the sink. She's delicious.

"Owen!" she objects, smacking my chest. "Stop it, we have company. Later." She winks.

"I don't care who sees me kiss you, but yes, ma'am. I'll let everyone know," I say, because she's the boss, but I pinch her plump ass when I walk by, which makes her squeal.

"Owen!" she repeats, and she and Drew both laugh and shake their heads. Drew gives me a high five as I walk by, and he stays in the kitchen to help Emerson.

Drew

Damn, that was one hell of a kiss. My face flushes a little, and I look down at my feet to try to hide it. It's been a while since my hose has been fully charged somewhere other than in my bunk room or the shower. I've known Owen and Emerson for a long time and, of course, I've seen them kiss before. It shouldn't affect me like this, but seeing him back her up against the counter made me a little jealous. Owen and Emerson are my friends. Hell, Owen is my best friend and they're happily married. No matter how hot they are, I need to distract myself.

"What else needs to be done?" I ask Emerson, shaking myself out of my reverie. She works hard as a teacher—more than forty hours a week—and takes up the slack at home from Owen working at the station all the time. I feel the need to take something off her plate; make things easier for her.

"Just eat all this food and relax. That's it," she tells me, with one of her gorgeous smiles. "Now grab a plate." Her long, brown hair is up in one of those messy buns, and damn if it isn't hard to keep from staring at her beautiful face. Owen is one lucky asshole.

I avert my eyes and don't hesitate grabbing food. I pile a plate high with a little of each of the delicious foods. Emerson is an excellent cook and I'm taking advantage of having something besides fast food for a change. I'll have to double my workout tomorrow to make up for it, but that's fine because Owen will have to double up, too, so he and his tattooed muscles can keep me company.

Just as I finish making my plate and grabbing a drink, everyone else walks in to get their food and the kitchen comes alive with talking, laughter, smiles, and hugs. I stick around to take it all in, nibbling on my food as I people watch.

Owen fills his plate with food and laughs at something Stathes says. Owen's got a great smile. I can see his back muscles flexing as he moves, and I can't help but think how lucky Emerson is to have him, too. Owen is a good man who works hard to do whatever he needs to for his family.

The kids fill their plates with mostly sweets and run off to their game room to eat in there. They used to call it their play room when they were younger, but Declan told me that's not a cool name for it now that they're older. Little does he know, he doesn't have to work hard to be cool. Declan is a great kid and we have fun together. I loved getting outside today and playing soccer with him and the guys. I'm going to pay for it tomorrow with some sore muscles, but it was worth it.

"Papciak, you having trouble there, bud?" I set my plate down and take the plate from him that he's trying to juggle while he's holding himself up on his crutches. "Let me help you." Although Cate is right there next to him, I'm the one that helps him get his food.

Lamont and Lauren eat at the table, but Lauren doesn't look happy. Lamont seems like he doesn't want to be here and now that I think back on it, I haven't heard him say a word to anyone today. I don't know them too well, so it's not my place to interfere. I give Lauren a small smile, which she returns, and I head to the living room where the other firefighters and Emerson are watching the game and eating.

Owen sits in his spot on the far side of the couch and Emerson, of course, sits in the middle next to him. Papciak and Cate take the loveseat, and I trade Nick his plate for his crutches and lean them up against the wall. I wonder how much love there actually is between Nick and Cate, because she didn't bother to help her boyfriend get his food even though he's on crutches. She doesn't seem like the nicest person I've ever met and she doesn't have much of a personality. She's cute, but he could easily do better. After meeting her today, I understand why she seemed to think Cecilia was so great when she had Nick set us up on that shitty blind date. Won't be doing that again.

Burrell and Stathes take two individual chairs to lounge in while they eat, so the only place left for me to sit is beside Emerson on the couch. I plop down beside her and place my drink on the table next to the couch. We're not extremely close to each other, but I can almost feel the heat coming off her and soaking into my skin. It makes me wish I had a woman like her to sit next to and put my arm around.

After my wife and son passed away during childbirth ten years ago, I withstood three years of self-imposed celibacy, but the guys at the station finally convinced me to dip my feet back in the ocean. I've dated here and there, but haven't found anyone I fit with for a long-term relationship. Hell if I'm going on any more blind dates. It's just easier to be alone. I spend most of my time at the station, anyway. Seeing how happy Owen and Emerson are together, it makes me wonder if I'll ever have someone to share my life with like that, or if I'll always be alone.

CHAPTER 5

WE EAT AND WATCH the game until our team makes a touchdown and all the guys are slapping high fives and shouting, "Woohoo! Yes! Alright!" We're a bunch of hooligans, and Emerson just shakes her head at us. Most wives would tell us to shut up, change the channel, but Emerson's hanging out right along with us and joining in on the fun. In fact, everyone seems to be having a great time except Lamont, so I venture over to him standing with his arms folded against the wall by the front door to see what's up.

"How you doing, Lamont? Are you a football fan?" I ask.

"Football is fine. I just have somewhere else I need to be. I told Lauren we could come for a little while but we need to get going." He stares straight at the TV, not that he's watching it, and never makes eye contact with me.

"If you need to head out, I can make sure Lauren and the kids get home safely. Would that help?" I hate for someone to be somewhere they don't want to be.

"Nah man, I'm not leaving Lauren here alone. God knows what'll happen. I'll give her a few more minutes, but then we're out of here."

"Okay, well, let me know if I can help." I wander back to my seat beside Emerson because at least she's...not being shitty.

At half time, Owen goes to check on the kids in the game room. Emerson goes to the kitchen to clean up, and I follow her to help. Polite guest and all that.

There's a comfortable silence between us while we're working together to clean the dishes, put the leftover food in the refrigerator, and wipe down the counters and stove. We leave the desserts out on the table for everyone to snack on. It takes almost no time to finish because we seem to be in sync with each other and what we need to do. When everything is done, her blue eyes find mine.

"Thanks for your help cleaning up, Drew. I appreciate not having to do it by myself." She smiles and looks down at the floor, but glances back up when I start talking.

"I don't mind a bit. Owen was with the kids, so he couldn't help. You guys made all that delicious food. I can at least help clean up. You shouldn't have to do things alone all the time and I know you have to because Owen works so much. The fire life is hard. I want you to know that I appreciate you inviting me over for the day. The food's been so much better than what I usually eat since I'm always at the station. It's been nice to just hang out with friends. You and Owen are lucky to have each other and your family."

I can't take my eyes off her and the two of us just stand there, gazing at one another. *What is she thinking?* I offer her a little smile and she returns it, but blushes a little and looks back at the floor.

The last thing I want to do is make her uncomfortable, so I walk over to her and put my arm around her shoulders like a friend would, saying, "C'mon. Let's get back to the game." She feels amazing under my arm, but we separate as we walk back into the living room to join the others in watching the rest of the game. After our team loses by three points, we all boo the television announcers and stand up to stretch.

Lamont says, "It's been great, but Lauren and I need to get back home. Thanks for inviting us over." He waits by the door with his arms folded while Lauren hugs Emerson, calls for their kids, and they head home on foot, carrying their closed umbrellas since the rain has stopped.

Papciak's girlfriend is clearly ready to leave, so he says, "I'll catch y'all at the station tomorrow," with a roll of his eyes. I overhear her ask him if she can listen to the radio traffic in the truck and can't help but wonder why she's so interested in hearing about our calls.

Burrell and Stathes are right behind them with Burrell's daughter. Burrell smacks Owen on the back and thanks Emerson for having them over.

Since it's just me and the Callaghan family now, I stand up from the couch and speak up, too. "I guess I'll be going. I probably need to get some laundry done before our shift starts tomorrow."

"Stay as long as you want. Hang out. There's no rush." Owen tells me.

Emerson nods her head. "Yeah, we'll probably watch a movie. You're welcome to stay and watch it, too. Plus, we still have all these snacks that didn't get eaten. Stay so I don't eat them all by myself." She pats her soft stomach like she's trying to make a statement.

"I don't see any reason why you couldn't eat them all by yourself, but sure, I'll stay for a while." I sit back down and Emerson grabs the remote to find a good movie to watch as she relaxes back in the middle of the couch between Owen and me.

I can't keep myself from imagining feeding her the bite-size brownies in the kitchen. I can almost imagine what her moans might sound like as she enjoys the fudgy chocolate. Owen can hold our glass of milk. I'm going to Hell in a handbasket.

Emerson

Owen and I cuddle on the couch, with Drew at the other end. We watch a movie while Keegan chats on the phone with her new boyfriend in her bedroom and Declan plays a video game online with his friends in the game room. I don't know if I'm imagining the feeling of someone watching me or if Drew is glancing at me now and then. I feel like he's watched me more than the movie. Don't get me wrong, he is a fine specimen of a man, but I'm happily married. A girl can look, though, can't she?

Owen is on my left side with his arm around me as I lean on him comfortably. Drew is a little farther away, relaxed on my other side, with his ankle up on his opposite knee. He's taller than Owen, has fewer tattoos on his arms, and has more hair since Owen shaves his head. His hair is dark brown—almost black—and is cut short on his neck while it flops down a little in front of his eyes. His face is clean-shaven like Owen's because the policy where they work mandates that they can't have facial hair. It all has to do with their fitted face masks. A beard or mustache would hinder the tight seal and the masks wouldn't fit correctly. I can't help but wonder what it might feel like to run my fingers through Drew's hair.

Suddenly, Drew looks in my direction and catches me looking at him. He gives me one of his sexy smiles with the dimple in his right cheek, but doesn't take his eyes off me. I smile back, but I have to be the one to break eye contact first, considering my husband is sitting right here with his arm around me. I can't imagine what he'd say if he caught Drew and me looking at each other.

Declan comes into the living room and plops down on the couch between me and Drew, like there's plenty of room when, really, he's half sitting on both of us.

"I'm bored," he whines.

"I thought you were playing video games?" I ask him.

"I was. Then, my friends had to go. I can't play that game by myself. What do I do now?"

Drew speaks up. "Would you mind if I come play a game or two with you? What are you playing?"

"Fortnite. That would be awesome if you could come play! I need help building a stronghold against the zombies." He and Drew go off down the hallway to the game room, leaving me alone with Owen.

Owen tightens his arm around me, saying, "Drew's a good friend to Declan. They're like two peas in a pod.

They'll probably be in there all night attacking zombies." He laughs.

"That's fine. I'm glad they can hang out. Drew's a terrific role model for Declan. It looks like it's just the two of us for the rest of the movie, though."

Owen doesn't try to hide the Cheshire Cat grin on his face. "I think I need to take advantage of this time while I can," he mumbles as he leans down to kiss me. What I thought would be an innocent peck turns into a panty-melting, sensual kiss that enthrals me. He cups my face with his brawny hands and runs his fingers through my hair, kissing his way from my lips along my jaw and up to my ear.

"I want you, Emerson," he whispers. "I've wanted you all day." His hand moves to my waist and slowly creeps under the elastic waistband of my leggings until his fingers reach the edge of those panties he's already melted off. He draws his fingers along the edge, teasing me as he kisses my neck, and a soft moan escapes me.

"Are you wet for me, Baby?" he whispers. He slides his finger under my panties to find me wet and ready for him, which elicits a sexy groan from this man I love.

"Mmm...you're soaking wet for me," he utters. He plays with my clit and then slides his finger inside of me. I can't keep quiet when he does this to me, so he puts his other hand over my mouth to stifle any noises that slip out. As if trying to keep quiet isn't already torture, he pulls his finger out, meets my needy gaze, then slides two fingers back inside of me.

"Is that what you want, Baby?" He whispers under his breath. He already knows the answer. I nod my head, then let it roll back on the couch as he feels the inside walls of my pussy, right where I want him to touch.

Suddenly, he steals his hand away from me and looks past me. I look up to see that Drew has come back down the hallway.

"Just grabbing a couple of drinks...don't mind me," he says, walking by with a chuckle. Our eyes meet and I can feel the flames burst from my cheeks as he grabs two drinks, winks at us, and goes back to the game room.

Owen drops his forehead to mine and we laugh silently together. Now that we've been discovered, we decide we'll just cuddle and watch the rest of the movie before we take our chances of getting caught by the kids.

Just as the credits for the movie start rolling, Drew cautiously comes back to the living room.

"Safe to enter?" he asks, with a smirk on his handsome face.

"Yeah, smartass, come on in. Show's over...in more ways than one," Owen says.

We hear tones go out to Owen's and Drew's fire station for a brush fire south of us. The dispatcher relays that flames are showing, and it's spreading quickly, but there are no injuries at this time.

"Do you guys need to go?" I ask.

"Nah," Owen replies. "There are plenty of guys on shift already. They'll take care of it." He yawns. "Excuse me. Damn, I'm tired. Maybe we should head to bed," he says with a wink of his eye that I'm sure Drew can clearly see.

"Yeah, me too," Drew says. "It's been a great day, guys. Thanks for having me over. It was nice to have a change of scenery."

We all stand and Drew shakes Owen's hand and pulls him a man hug while they pound each other on the back. Drew then hugs me tightly—for a little too long?—with an almost imperceptible rub of his hand on my back. His embrace is warm and feels comfortable to me, so I feel a tiny shiver when he lets me go.

"I'll see you guys later. Have fun tonight," he says as he winks at both of us and dashes out to his truck in the darkness.

Owen closes the front door, locks it, and takes my hand. "I have to say, I got a little jealous when Drew was hugging you. Was it just me, or was that kind of a long hug?"

"Pffttt...I think it was just you. Or maybe his hug with *you* was kind of a long hug?" I raise an eyebrow in question. "Drew is our friend. I'm sure it was innocent. Now, are we headed to bed?"

Chapter 6

Emerson

OWEN SMILES SLYLY, MOVING closer to me, so his chest is pressed against mine. He looks down at me, tilts my chin up, and rumbles, "I've been waiting for you all day long. You go get ready for bed. I'll lock up and meet you in the bedroom." He brushes his lips against mine, giving me a little taste of things to come.

I say a quick goodnight to the kids in their bedrooms. "Don't stay up too late," I tell Keegan and I notice she looks upset. I step into her room and ask if she's okay, but she just nods, rolls over, and disappears under the covers. I give her a big squeeze to let her know I'm here for her. Maybe we need to have some girl time soon. Since we're on Winter Break, we should be able to find some time to do something fun. This is time for all of us to relax and unwind so we can start the year fresh with renewed energy.

Or at least, I hope so. January can be a tough month for both students and teachers.

I stop in Declan's room and he's building something with Lego bricks, even though he was supposed to be in bed half an hour ago. "Declan, it's time to get to bed."

"I'm not tired. I can't go to sleep."

"It's past your bedtime and you need to get sleep so you can have a good day tomorrow."

"Why do I have to go to bed early, anyway? It's not a school night." He immediately starts his usual debate about bedtime. "You know, we don't really need eight hours of sleep every night, and I can sleep late in the morning. I saw this TikTok video with a guy who was a doctor and he said..."

"Declan, go to sleep. You can't believe everything you see on the Internet."

"But Mom, he said that the less sleep you get, the better your brain will think tomorrow because it goes into survival mode. Do you know what survival mode is? Survival mode happens when you..."

"Yes, Declan. Survival mode is what you'll be in if you don't go to sleep." All I can do is roll my eyes at this kid. "Declan, I'm not having the bedtime debate with you again. I know it's not a school night, but you still need to get some sleep. We need to stick close to our schedule or it will be hard to get back into it when break is over. We've already let you stay up later than you normally go to bed. Try reading a book, doing a meditation, or something else to calm your mind. Good night. I love you," I say, closing the door.

It's hard for his ADHD brain to slow down at night and relax. It's so much more than a lack of attention and hyperactivity. He struggles with so many things in life that it makes my heart hurt. We are constantly trying to help him learn ways to outsmart the coexisting conditions and symptoms that come along with ADHD.

I head to the other end of the hallway to my bedroom and get ready for bed. I can still hear banging upstairs as Declan continues to build with Legos. I don't know what I'm going to do with that kid. I know what I won't be doing. You've got to pick your battles. This one is not one I'm going to fight tonight. I'll let him have this minor victory since he's right. It's not a school night.

After choosing a cute pajama set, I make my way into the shower and turn on the water. I undress, turn on some calming music on my phone, and step in. The hot water sluicing down my shoulders and back feels incredible after a long day. When I'm fully soaked, I massage some shampoo into my hair and scalp. I'm almost finished washing my hair when the shower curtain moves and startles me. Owen pokes his head in. "Mind if I join you?" He grins that handsome grin of his and steps in before I can even answer.

"Sure, be my guest, since you weren't going to wait for an answer anyway," I reply facetiously. I notice he's only been in the shower for two seconds, but he's already hard with expectation.

"Gotta save water and help the Earth, you know." He stands close in front of me so our bodies are touching and he can take over rinsing my hair. It feels heavenly when he massages my scalp and runs his fingers through my hair to remove the shampoo. I close my eyes and revel in his touch.

"Yeah, I'm sure your entire reasoning for being in here with me is to save the Earth," I counter as he adds conditioner to his palm and massages it through my hair with both hands. I can't help but sigh at the feeling his caress evokes in me. It's such a platonic thing, washing and conditioning my hair, but it feels so intimate. It's not something just anyone would do for you. Once he's done distributing the conditioner through my hair, he rinses it out just as thoroughly.

I grab the soap and lather every inch of his body so that he's covered in bubbles, then use the handheld showerhead to rinse him off. He grabs my pouf, adds my body wash to it, and repeats the favor for me, paying extra attention to my boobs. After he rinses the bubbles from my skin, he moves the handheld showerhead down to spray between my legs to tease me and then hangs it back up.

He smiles and melds his naked body to mine as he wraps his arms around me and kisses me with a groan, pressing his body against mine so I can feel just how much he wants me. "You're so gorgeous. I love your body. Drew's right; I'm a lucky man."

Wait a minute. Did Drew tell him that? Did he hear Drew say that to me? Owen wasn't in the kitchen when we were talking.

I must have a pensive look on my face because he says, "Yeah, I heard Drew tell you we were lucky to have each other."

"Were you spying on us while we cleaned the kitchen?" I ask just for kicks.

"I wasn't spying...just happened to walk by the kitchen after checking on the kids today. He couldn't take his eyes off you. I can't blame him, but he better be careful. He tells me all the time how lucky I am to have such a gorgeous, smart wife. And he's so right, but...You. Are. Mine." He kisses me hard, his tongue gliding in to caress mine as his fingers tangle in my hair tightly. I don't know if my nipples pebbling are from his chest rubbing against them or from thinking about my conversation with Drew this afternoon.

When the kiss comes to an end, I draw in a deep breath and look into Owen's mesmerizing eyes and tell him, "You have nothing to worry about, Owen. I love you and I'll always be yours."

"Damn straight," he adds. And he proceeds to stake his claim on his territory. The sensual moans and groans coming from the shower must sound like a rated X movie. Thank goodness our master suite is on the opposite end of the house from the kids' bedrooms.

He bends down, reaches behind my thighs and lifts me up to press me against the shower wall. His mouth is all over my neck and breasts as he lowers me down onto his rigid dick, right where I want him. I hold on to his neck, wrap my legs around him, and he pumps into me over and over as hard as he can. We're both panting so heavily that we can't speak. I hear the low growl coming from Owen's chest, and I know he's about to come inside of me.

"Owen, come in me, Honey. I want to feel you throbbing in my pussy."

And he does. He lets go with a rumble that resembles intense thunder on a dark night and hugs me tightly to his chest. We hold each other until the hot water starts to turn warm and he slowly slides me down his body to my feet. He rinses us both again with the handheld showerhead before the water gets too cold, turns off the water, and dries my skin with my towel. Then Owen dries himself while I enjoy the view of his muscled back and legs and we go to bed sans clothing.

Laying down under the covers, we get comfortable and snuggle together for a few minutes before he says, "Your turn." He knows sometimes it's difficult for a woman to have an orgasm, but he never wants to let me go without. I love him for that.

"Owen, you don't have..." Before I can finish, he pulls the covers up over his head and meanders his way slowly down my body with soft touches, kisses, and licks until he reaches the crease between my legs. He hovers there for a moment, making me wait, and the anticipation of his hot breath turning into a wet stroke of his tongue makes me run my fingers over his smooth head and squeeze. Owen chuckles and licks his wide tongue from my ass up to my clit, making me moan and squirm in the most sensual pleasure. He tastes every part of me from my clit, to between the folds of my lips, until he finally reaches my opening and swirls his tongue around mercilessly.

"Owen," I whimper, "your mouth feels so incredible."

"Mmhmm," he murmurs his thanks—or agreement, I'm not sure—then moves his mouth up to suck my clit and shoves two fingers into me as deep as they'll go. He pumps them in and out of me, wet noises and my pleasurable whimpers filling the air around us as he continues to take my clit into his mouth. When he reaches up to pinch my nipple, I finally lose it, my insides clenching tight as I exhale with an arousing groan. I squeeze his shoulders and my hips buck up involuntarily. He is relentless, giving as much as I need until I float back down from the clouds and he holds me in his arms. Together, our heartbeats slow to their regular rhythm and our eyes begin to close. He may be gone at work most of the time, and I miss him immensely when he's not here, but damn, does he make up for it when he comes home.

Chapter 7

Drew

At 6:00am, my alarm screams, but it's too late. I'm already frustratingly awake, laying in bed, putting off getting ready for work. I stayed at the station last night because there was an open rack, but I could barely sleep. When I did, it was filled with dreams of me being alone or me with a woman who I couldn't quite recognize.

When I left the Callaghan house last night, it was clear what Owen and Emerson would be up to that night. Owen nonchalantly mentioned he was ready for bed, but I know what he wanted. He even had a little pregame show that I didn't mind accidentally walking in on. With a wife as gorgeous as Emerson, I'd want to devour her, too.

Hell, I think I do want that, and she's not even my wife. What kind of friend am I? I'd never come between the two of them. They have such a great relationship that it almost seems perfect. Maybe Emerson has a single friend. One with a nice body and thick thighs like Emerson's.

Great, now I'm getting hard. Every time I woke up last night, I had a hard-on. There's no way I can make it through the day with blue balls like this. I think about those dreams with the woman whose face I couldn't see. I close my eyes and wonder what her face looked like. Her body was incredibly full and luscious.

Remembering the dream when she confidently walked up to me, put her arms around my neck, and pressed her body to mine, I slide my hand down to my shorts. Pulling my dick out, I massage it like I want my dream girl to do. My other hand reaches down to stroke my balls. In my mind, my dream girl straddles me and slides down on me, her tight, wet pussy squeezing my dick while she glides up and down on it. I come on my stomach, doing my best to stay quiet so no one hears me. The last thing I need is the guys ragging on me for beating off over a dream I had. Shaking myself back into reality, I get up to shower and head downstairs to begin my overtime shift.

Owen and Captain Wiershen are already sitting in the day room eating breakfast when I get down there. Kounovsky and Delgado are there on their regular shift. Captain is giving out duties for the day and previewing who will most likely have to work overtime next shift. She stops in her tracks when she hears the tones on the loudspeaker.

"Engine 41, Brush 42, Tanker 46, respond to the area of 5923 Waters Edge Circle for a report of a rekindled brush fire." Dispatch goes on to repeat the information as we're throwing on our gear and jumping on the trucks. It sounds like the marsh fire must have started back up. The guys thought they got it out when they handled it yesterday, but one little spark can light it off again. It's probably the farmers who grow asparagus down in that area. They burn the asparagus with a controlled burn to help the next crop grow in, but sometimes it gets out of hand. It's an old-fashioned concept, but hey, they're an old-fashioned bunch down that way.

When we arrive on scene, we realize the fire is much bigger than it was yesterday. Not only did it relight, but it's spread over a few acres of land. Our first arriving unit, which happens to be the Captain, assumes command and communicates a scene size-up over the radio. She instructs each unit on where to go and what to do and we take care of business.

It's a rough day with high winds and cold temperatures. As soon as we cut a firebreak and think we've got it under control, embers float on the gusts of wind and start new fires. We work to douse the flames and hours later, our exhausted fire crew returns to the station to wash the trucks and equipment, get our turnout gear cleaned, and take showers.

We missed lunch, so everyone is starving for dinner and some sleep. We place a huge Chinese food order and scarf it down before the tones go out again.

"Engine 41, Medic 44, respond to 152 Church Lane for a report of a heart attack in progress." Damn, the guys on Engine 41 are pissed. They barely got their food down and now they have to respond to a medical call.

"Sorry 'bout your luck! We'll eat your dessert for ya!" I shout as they're running to the trucks. The rest of the crew laugh their asses off, mostly because they're so tired any damn thing would be funny right now. Thank God we didn't have to go back out. Those guys are going to be wore the fuck out. The rest of us head off to our racks to get some sleep before we get those midnight tones that are always inevitable. As we go up, Owen is ahead of me on the stairs, and I see nothing but his muscular calves.

"Owen, you gonna work out tonight? We missed our usual time when we were on that call earlier." I'm tired as hell, but if he's working out, I'll join him. It's easier, somehow, when you have a friend to work out with.

"Nah, I think the call was enough of a workout for today. Let's hit the gym tomorrow." I nod as he gives me a fist bump and we amble on to our bunks for the night.

Hanging out in my bunk room watching TV, my mind wanders back to last night's dreams. Hopefully, tonight's dreams have more of the good stuff and less of the lonely stuff. I don't want to think about being alone for the rest of my life, talking to my cat and yelling at the television. I need to get out there somehow, and meet someone new. How I'll do that is a mystery since I'm constantly working at a fire station—whether it be paid or volunteer. My personal life is almost nonexistent and it'll stay that way unless I make a change. I drift off to sleep, thinking about what my perfect woman would be like. Frustratingly enough, she has wavy brown hair, mystical blue eyes, a caring heart, and a curvaceous body to die for. I just might.

Emerson

Owen's been at the station for a couple of days now. He sent a text message saying they've not only been running their regular emergency calls, they've also been repeatedly responding to the same brush fire. They even had to call in other surrounding counties because it spread even more than it already had. It's almost strange how it's happening, like there's some force behind the fire making it spread.

The kids are enjoying Winter Break, but Declan needs to get outside and get active. Yesterday he had a meltdown because Keegan ate the last blueberry muffin, even though he ate the other three late at night when we were all sleeping. He couldn't just eat the blueberry yogurt we have instead because he doesn't like the texture. His ADHD comes with so many facets that it's like raising multiple children even though we only have one Declan. It can get tiring sometimes, but I know it's even more frustrating for him having to deal with these things. His counselor, Owen, and I are trying to teach him some strategies to get past the things that wear him down.

Keegan has been moody for the past few days. I took her to the nail spa to get our nails done, but she didn't open up to me. I think she's upset about a boyfriend problem. Maybe she can talk to her Dad when he comes home from work. He'll have some good advice for her. It was still good to spend some time with her. Our schedules are so busy that it's rare that we get to do that. Once school starts back up, it'll be chaotic again.

The kids have dentist appointments today, so I'm headed to get ready for the day. I need to shower and get them moving so we can get there on time. I pick out a comfy, yet cute outfit and jump in the shower. The hot water feels good on my tired muscles. Enjoying the warmth, I get some shampoo to wash my hair.

"Ahhhhh!" The water suddenly freezes me into an icicle. What the hell? The hot water heater must have died. I knew it was coming, but didn't think it would happen so soon. There's always something breaking, and always at the wrong time. I get out of the shower and get dressed. My wet hair is in a bun on top of my head and it looks like that's as fancy as it's getting today. I call Owen on his cell. He picks up after six rings, breathing heavy.

"Hey, Babe. Can't really talk right now. I'm on a call. What's up?"

"I'm sorry. I have a situation and I was going to see if you could come home and either take the kids to the dentist or fix the water heater while I take them."

"Damn. I can't. We're on the way to the hospital with a patient." He thinks for a moment. "Let me call Drew and see if he can help you. He's off today and hanging out at Stathes' house."

"That'd be great if he could. Thanks, Honey." I wait for him to text me an update while I explain to the kids that there is no hot water, but yet, they still need to get ready to go. I don't want to pay a no show fee for two dentist appointments. After a few minutes, a text comes through.

Owen

> I called Drew. He's on his way to help.

Emerson

> Thanks. I appreciate it. We'll get it taken care of. Be safe.

About twenty minutes go by and I hear Drew's truck pulling into the driveway. When he walks through the door, Keegan is ready to head to the dentist, but Declan has barricaded himself in his bedroom.

I greet him with an exhausted sigh and a hug, saying, "Hi Drew, thank you for coming to help."

"Of course. Anytime," he says with a smile, like he really means it.

"Do you know anything about water heaters? Ours stopped working. Keegan and Declan have dentist appointments to get to. Declan refuses to come out of his room and I don't know why."

"What can I do?"

"Well, first we have to get Declan out of his room and calmed down. Then, maybe you could take a look at the water heater while I take the kids to the dentist, or vice versa. Either way is fine with me."

"Why don't you and Keegan go relax in the living room? I'll go talk to Declan." He heads to Declan's room and I can hear him knock on the door. I'm doubtful that he will be able to help. Declan knows him, but rarely is he willing to talk to anyone besides me or Owen.

CHAPTER 8

Drew

"DECLAN? YOU OKAY BUD?" I wait for him to answer, but I get nothing in return. I knock again before trying the handle. Locked.

"Hey Declan, you've got to go to the dentist and you guys are going to be late if you don't come out. Do you want to tell me what you're thinking?" I wait another minute. Then I hear the door unlock. He slowly opens it an inch, just enough to see through the crack, then goes to sit on his bed.

"Can I come in?" When he says yes, I sit beside him on the bed, but give him some space so I don't make him feel more overwhelmed. "What's happening? You okay? You've got your mom and sister worried about you."

He hesitates like he wants to talk to me, but he's not quite sure. With a red face, he grits out, "I hate the dentist. I hate the water heater. I hate everything."

"Well, I have good news. We're going to fix the water heater. Is that why you're overwhelmed right now?"

"Yeah, I was supposed to take a shower before going to the dentist and now I can't. Now I have to go without a shower and it feels weird."

"Yeah, I hate when plans change, too. We'll get that taken care of so you can get back to your regular schedule, Buddy. I promise. We do need to get you to the dentist in the meantime. Would you rather me take you and Keegan or your mom take you guys? You can choose." I'm hoping putting the ball in his court will help him feel better, like he has a little control over a seemingly chaotic situation. I can tell he's debating in his head whether to pick me or his mom for a ride there.

"You. But only if I get to choose the radio station and ride up front," he mumbles.

"Okay, but I get to veto any stations I think are inappropriate. Deal?" I put my hand out to shake his like we're making an old-fashioned agreement.

"Deal," he says, and shakes my hand before heading out of his bedroom door, down the hall, and out the front door without a word to anyone else.

I head to the living room and Emerson is amazed that he came out of his room so quickly.

"What did you say to him? I didn't think he would come out," she says, shocked.

"I just promised him that we would get the water heater fixed so he could get back to his regular routine. Then I let him choose which one of us will take him to the dentist. He wants me to take them, but the caveat is that Declan gets to ride up front and pick the music." I look at Keegan and raise an eyebrow to ask if that's okay with her. She nods.

"Well, okay then! Wow. Thanks. Are you sure you really don't mind taking them?" Emerson has a worried look on her face.

"I don't mind at all. How about you get to work on that water heater and we'll see you when we get home?" Home. This isn't my home, but she knows what I meant. "If you're still working on it when we get back, I can help you."

A sigh of relief escapes her lips. "Sounds like a plan. Thank you, Drew." She raises up on her toes to give me another hug and we head out the door.

On the ride there, Declan picks some crazy ass funky pop station to listen to. What the hell, it's only a thirty-minute drive. I can handle that if it helps my friend and his family. Keegan's in the backseat texting with someone and has an angry look on her face. I hate to see her upset. *Maybe I can ask her about it when I get a chance, just to make sure she's okay.* We pull up to the brick building, check in with the front desk receptionist, and find seats in the waiting room. Declan seems to be doing fine, almost as if nothing out of the ordinary ever happened.

A lady in blue scrubs pokes her head into the waiting room. "Declan Callaghan? We're ready for you, Sweetheart."

I look at Declan to see if he's okay going by himself and he gives me a thumbs up like he's doing just fine. Now it's just me and Keegan in the waiting room, and she finally put her phone away.

"Hey K, I noticed you seemed a little upset in the truck on the way here. Everything okay?" I ask.

After a heavy sigh, she says, "Yeah. I guess. Just texting with someone and they're being stupid."

"Oh, I know stupid. Remember where I work?" She laughs. "If you ever need to talk about anything or you want a sounding board with someone who's not your Mom or Dad, I'm happy to listen. Been known to give good advice a time or two." I give her a smirk and she smiles back at me.

"Thanks, Drew. I just don't really know what to do. There's this guy that says he likes me and he texts me all the time, but when we're in school, he doesn't want to talk to me or be seen with me. I don't get it. If he likes me, why won't he talk to me in person?"

"Have you asked him about it? That's always the best thing to do first. Communication is a major part of a good relationship." She shakes her head no. "I would suggest finding time to talk to him about it then. See what he says." She nods in agreement and I put my arm around her for a little squeeze. Then the same lady in blue scrubs comes back to get Keegan.

"Keegan, we're ready for you. Your brother is just about finished." Keegan walks back with her and I'm left alone in the waiting room while they get their teeth cleaned.

I wonder how Emerson is doing with the water heater and if she's fixed it or if I can help her when we get back. She is one of the strongest women I know. She reminds me a lot of Corinne. They're both intelligent, caring, beautiful, and great with kids.

Declan comes walking back into the waiting room, jerking me out of my reverie, and I ask him, "How'd it go?"

He says, "Good. Thanks for letting me go back by myself. Mom never lets me. I guess she thinks I'm still a baby and can't go alone. The lady said my teeth look good, but that I need to floss more. The dentist said I don't have any cavities."

"Sounds like a good report to me. Awesome. We'll just hang out and wait for Keegan, and then we'll head back home to see your Mom. How's soccer going?"

"It's alright. Coach Alex is making me play forward, but I'd rather be a defender. It sucks."

"Can you talk to the coach about it?"

"I could, but he wants us to try all the positions, so it probably won't help."

"That might not be a bad idea. If you learn what to do in all the different positions, you'll be better equipped to work as a team later when you do find a position you want to stay in. As a defender, you'll know what the forward needs to work together to score a goal or defend against the other team."

He looks pensive. "I hadn't thought about it like that before. I guess you're right. I still hate it, though."

"Well, don't give up on it just because you have to try other positions. You're a skilled soccer player. Your team's lucky to have you." He blushes a little and looks out the window, so we sit in comfortable silence.

When Keegan is finished with the dentist, we all pile into the truck and about half an hour later, we're pulling into the driveway at home. We walk in the front door and smell something delicious.

"Hey guys! You're back already. That didn't take long. What did the dentist say?" Emerson asks as we stroll through the door.

"Good reports for both Declan and Keegan. Although Declan needs to floss more," I tell her.

"Sounds good. Thank you so much for taking them to their appointments, Drew. I was able to get the water heater fixed. The bottom heating element crapped out. Too much sediment buildup, so it overheated. Luckily, the hardware store had one in stock. I was able to replace it and we're back up and running again. I thought I'd go ahead and get dinner started so that you guys could eat when you got back. Will you stay for dinner? As a thank you for helping us today?" She looks at me with hopeful blue eyes and I can't say no.

"I'll stay, but only on one condition." Her eyebrows raise up with curiosity. "You have to let me help you cook." I think she's a little surprised that I want to help her, which makes me smile. "Hey, I can cook! I know my way around a kitchen. Let me help you. The kids can set the table. Less work for you."

"Well, okay then. Let's cook!" she says with her adorable smile.

"Why do I have to set the table? I have to do everything!" Declan whines.

"I'll help you, dweeb. It's not a big deal. Just grab the napkins," Keegan says. I give her a fist bump to say thank you.

Declan, reluctantly, and Keegan get started setting the table, while Emerson and I cook. While I'm cutting up some vegetables, she texts Owen to let him know everything is taken care of and the family is back on track.

We finish cooking and set everything on the table. The four of us eat together like a family would. It's been forever since I sat and had a nice dinner with anyone that resembled family. Corinne was a wonderful cook, and we always sat together to talk about our day and make plans for the future. It took a lot of time in counseling for me to be able to get past losing her and move on, but I know she would want that. She wouldn't want me to be alone and unhappy. That's the type of person she was.

We enjoy our delicious dinner together and start to clean up. With all four of us helping clear the table, it doesn't take long. I'm not sure if the kids have chores or not, but I figure I'll put a bug in their ear.

"Keegan, Declan, what do you say you guys take care of the dishes while your mom rests?" To my surprise, and I think to Emerson's surprise as well, they agree. They're great kids.

Emerson and I walk to the living room and I let her choose her seat first. She sits on the couch, so I sit on the loveseat across from her, just to be on the safe side. I enjoy her company while we talk about the fire station, her job, and their plans for their school break, which brings the conversation back around to the kids.

"I can't believe you got them to do the dishes!" she says, amused.

"Why wouldn't they?"

"I can ask them to do something and it's like pulling teeth. It's just too much to ask. You or Owen ask, and they jump right on it. I don't get it." She shakes her head.

"I think it has to do with you being their mom; their safe place. Kids know they can do anything—or not do any-thing—and you'll still love them, no matter what. They know their Dad will, too, but it's always different with Mom. They probably tend to take advantage of you. I think if you talk to them about it and let them know how much it would help you for them to do more around the house, they would be more willing to help out. Maybe you could set up certain chores for certain days. Just a thought. They're great kids." I hope she doesn't get mad at me for giving her parenting advice.

"It's a terrific thought. I'll try it. I'd love some help around the house. With Owen gone all the time, I feel like I'm working my full-time job, plus being two parents at once. You are really great with the kids. You should have kids of your own."

"To be honest, I did." She looks at me in shock. "I don't tell too many people this, but I was married about 13 years ago and we got pregnant with our son, Michael, about ten years ago. We were thrilled to be starting a family. Then, when Corinne was two months along, we found out she had pancreatic cancer. The doctors worked with us intricately to make sure Cori and Michael had a safe pregnancy and delivery, but despite their efforts and ours, she went into labor two months early and I lost both of them." I'm shocked at myself for telling her this. It's just the two of us and now that I've stopped talking, it is eerily silent, except for a clink here and there coming from the kitchen.

"Andrew! You've never told me that." She has tears in her eyes. "I'm so sorry to hear you went through that. It can't be easy for you, especially being around other families."

"Sometimes it is hard, but it actually helps me to be around your family. Declan is about the same age Michael would be if he were still here with me. I think that's why I enjoy spending time with Declan. You all are such a great team that it makes me think about what it could be like to have a family. To maybe try again."

"I'm so glad you shared that with me. Are you ready to try again? Start dating, I mean?"

"Sure. The guys at the station back in Illinois let me go three years before they started hassling me to go out again. Between them and my therapist, I was able to make progress and I've gone on dates here and there. I just had a blind date not too long ago that was terrifying. Nobody has come along that I felt interested in a future with. We'd go on a couple of dates, and then we'd see that we weren't meant for each other, so we moved on amicably. Except for this one woman. She came to the station looking for me so often after we called it off that the Chief had to ask her to leave the premises and not come back." That makes her pretty smile appear on her face and she laughs.

"Well, I can't say I blame her. You are a catch." She blushes a little and I decide that she's even more beautiful with a little pink in her cheeks.

"I should probably be going. That is, if there's nothing else I can help you with before I go," I say, heading to the door. Emerson walks with me.

"No, I couldn't possibly ask you to do anything else. You've helped so much and it's turned out to be a pretty great day, despite the struggles we've had. Thank you so much, Drew." She puts her arms around my waist, presses her cheek to my chest to hug me with her hands flat on my back, and I hug her back tightly.

Looking down at her in my arms, I quietly—for her ears only—tell her, "If you don't mind me saying so, Emerson, Owen and the kids are so fortunate to have such a capable, clever, beautiful woman in their lives."

She blushes again and simply says, "Thank you. That is very sweet of you to say."

"Just the truth," I say, looking into her eyes. I step back, unwillingly leaving her warm embrace. "I'll see you soon. Good night."

Halfway to my truck, I turn around simply because I want to see her one more time. I smile and wave to her as she stands on the front porch. Trudging on, I try to remind myself that I'm climbing into bed alone tonight and not with that perfect woman I just walked away from. Best night I've had in a long time. Makes it hard to leave.

CHAPTER 9

"I SHOULD PROBABLY BE going. That is, if there's nothing else I can help you with before I go," Drew said tonight.

Oh, the things I could think of for him to help me with.

C'mon, Emerson, get your mind out of the gutter. You're married.

Today started out awful with the hot water heater dying on me and then Declan refused to come out of his room so we could go to the dentist. To make things worse, Owen couldn't help me. Life can get really stressful when you're parenting at home alone, especially when your husband works shift work. I remind myself that I should be thankful. I could be a single mom, trying to make ends meet on my own. I couldn't imagine how much worse that would be.

Luckily, Drew saved the day and came over to help. He's always been the first one to step up when we need a friend. Whether it's Owen needing a hand fixing one of the vehicles, me needing help with the kids or the house, or the kids needing help with a school project, Drew is always there. I still can't believe he got Declan to come out of his room so quickly. He's so good with Declan. Drew taking the kids to the dentist for me so I could work on the water heater was such a huge help.

I almost didn't want him to leave tonight.

I wish there was a way I could repay him.

I know exactly how I'd like to repay him.

I could have walked him out to his truck tonight.

Maybe I'd have said something like, "I really appreciate all that you do for us, Drew."

He'd respond with a dimpled smile and his usual, "I don't mind at all, Emerson. I'm happy to help."

Standing beside his lifted truck, I would ask, "Is there anything I can do for you?"

"You don't owe me anything, Sweetheart."

"You're a single guy and you said you were dating, but haven't found anyone. Maybe I could help you relax a little since it's been a while."

He'd hop up into his truck, saying, "Um, Emerson, you're..."

"I know, but you help us so much. Let me help you." He'd look down at me with his gorgeous blue eyes.

With one foot on the gas pedal like he's ready to go and one leg still hanging out of the truck, he'd cautiously venture, "How, exactly, would you like to help me, Emerson?"

His waist would be right at my eye level, and I'd reach over to unbuckle his belt. He'd hesitantly lean back so I could unbutton his pants and pull down his zipper.

"Are you sure about this, Emerson?" He'd never want to ruin his friendship with Owen.

I'd offer him no answer as I'd reach in his pants and feel his dick for the first time. He would be hard. And thick. Maybe I'd barely be able to put my fingers around him. I'd pull him out of his pants, licking my lips as I wrap my mouth around him. I'd feel him get even harder as I'd slide my mouth down his shaft and massage his base with my hand.

A groan would seductively fill the air as I'd suck his dick. He'd begin to run his fingers through my hair, finally giving in to what I want to do for him. He would feel so good on my tongue that I'd moan in pleasure, sending vibrations along his shaft, and he would rumble my name.

"Emerson..."

I'd take him in my mouth as deep as I could, then slide off him. He would feel so good filling up my mouth that I wouldn't be able to restrain myself. I would begin to speed up and so would our breathing. His fingers would grasp my hair just tight enough to make it hurt perfectly.

"Fuck, Emerson, that feels so good. You're gonna make me come."

I'd pull him out of my mouth long enough to look up at him and say, "Please. I want to feel you come in my mouth. I want to taste you." I'd suck him back into my mouth so hard my cheeks hollow with the pressure, glancing up at him to see the pleasure on his face and...

"Aw, fuck..." he'd mumble and let go, gripping my hair tighter. I'd be able to feel him throbbing as streams of come fill my mouth and I drink them down. When he's finished, I'd lick his dick to clean him up, wipe my mouth, and look back up at him.

The look on Drew's face would tell me I've adequately paid him back.

A creaking door behind me startles me out of my fantasy.

"Mom, can I have some ice cream?" Declan asks.

It takes me a second to switch gears. I blink a few times and finally register what he said. "Um, yeah, Honey. That's fine. Have some ice cream." *Maybe we should all have some ice cream. No, I think I need a cold shower instead.*

I follow him inside and as he goes to the kitchen, I slip down the hall to my bedroom and close the door. Locking it for good measure, I start the shower and undress. A cold shower is probably just the thing I need to clear my mind, but the hot water feels so good running down my body. I can still see Drew in my mind, sitting in front of me in the truck and tugging on my hair. My hand slides down on its own to feel my pussy and fuck, I'm soaking wet.

I'd never cheat on my husband, but damn, if I had the opportunity to be with both of them, I'd go for it in a heartbeat. What a wild fantasy! I've never done anything like that before, but a girl can dream, right? Especially when my husband is on shift and isn't here to help me out.

My mind wanders to Owen and Drew as I slide my cool fingers down my body, from my neck to my breasts, to my warm folds, and finger my clit like they would if dreams really could come true. I reach up with one hand to massage my breast while I'm feeling myself between my legs. I dip one finger into my pussy and it feels so good that I add another finger to make it feel like it's either Owen's or Drew's dick sliding into me.

The hot water runs down my skin as my fingers work faster and faster; harder and rougher, as though my two men were taking me. I pinch and pull on my nipple and it sends a shock through my core to my wet pussy that makes my stomach clench as I come.

Wow. That was intense.

I wash my body, shampoo and condition my hair, and dry off. Rubbing my patchouli and lavender lotion all over my sensitive body, I can imagine myself sleeping soundly tonight after that little workout.

First, however, parental duties call, so I have to get the kids off to bed. Once I'm dressed in my pajamas and my heartbeat has returned to normal, I venture into the living room.

"Hey guys, it's time to head to bed," I tell them.

"Mom," Keegan whines, "It's not even that late. Why do I have to go to bed at the same time as Declan?"

"Keegan, I want you to get some good rest. You don't have to go right to sleep, Sweetie, but at least go lay in bed and relax so you can fall asleep soon."

"I'm not a kid anymore. Why do you treat me like a kid?"

"Keegan, this isn't like you, hun. What's going on? Is something wrong?" I sit beside her on the couch and rub her back, which seems to help her relax.

"It's just been a crappy day. I don't mean to take it out on you. I have a huge project due in a few days and my group isn't exactly working together. It's *that* time of the month, and this guy I like is being stupid. He talks to me sometimes, but not at other times. I can't figure it out."

"Have you tried talking to him? Communication is important in a relationship."

She rolls her eyes at me. *I'm going to let that one go because she's had a bad day.*

"We're not in a relationship, Mom. Besides, Drew said that same thing, and I'm going to try to talk to the guy tomorrow."

"You talked to Drew about a guy? When? What did he say?"

"At the dentist today. He said what you said. That communication is really important in a relationship and I need to talk to him."

"Drew's a clever guy, isn't he?"

"Yeah. I like him."

"Me, too. He's a great friend," I tell her. After a moment, I ask, "Keegan, this guy you like...what kind of guy is he?"

"I don't know. He plays football. He's cute."

"Is he nice to you? Respectful to you? Because you deserve that," I tell her in earnest.

She thinks for a minute before answering. "I guess I don't even see him often enough to know if he's respectful to me."

"Hmm," is all I can say about that. "Keegan, what kind of guy would you like to date? I think if you know your answer to that, it would help you with this situation."

Pensively, she says, "A guy that respects me, treats me like a friend, opens doors for me, and isn't afraid to be seen with me in public. Someone who is proud of me like Dad is proud of you. Maybe a guy who listens to me and cares, like Drew listened to me today."

"Does knowing that put things in perspective for you?"

Keegan nods, saying, "Thanks, Mom." She gives me a hug and saunters off to her bedroom. I can't believe she talked to Drew about a boyfriend, but not me. At least she still hugged me. I have no doubt she'll just text with someone on her phone until she falls asleep.

Declan, on the other hand, has fallen asleep on the couch. I decide to just leave him there, covering him up with his Minecraft blanket and turning out the lights and TV. I clean up his ice cream bowl and put the ice cream that he left on the counter back into the freezer.

A yawn escapes me as I lock the doors. It seems as though we've all had a long, draining day and could use a good night's sleep.

CHAPTER 10

Owen

I DON'T KNOW WHAT I'd have done if Drew couldn't go help Emerson the other day. Emerson said he even helped when Declan was about to have a meltdown. That shocked me because usually, Declan will only talk with me or Emerson. Drew's been around for a while as a family friend, though, so I suppose he's grown on all of us.

I'm hanging out at home today on a much-needed day off. It's too quiet in the house now that Emerson and the kids have gone back to school. Winter Break always seems to go by too fast because I'm at work a good portion of the time, so even though they were home for two weeks, I only got to see them for four days. It was nice having them home when I was home from work. I'm usually by myself while they're in school. I miss spending time with them.

We did manage to find time to visit the aquarium one day, and another day, we saw a movie that the kids enjoyed. It reminded me that I really need to take Emerson out for a real date soon. It's been so long since I've spoiled her, and I've learned that you have to work at your marriage if you want it to work.

Today, I'm taking care of all those things I can't get to when I'm at work. On the agenda today is cutting and stacking firewood, changing the oil in my truck, and taking care of some laundry. I try to help as much as I can when I am home since I'm gone so much. Emerson says we need to hire a cleaning lady or someone to help around the house. I agree, that would be nice, but we can't really afford it.

When my phone rings, I notice Drew's name on the caller ID. "Hey man, what's up?"

"Hanging out at the volunteer station, but not much is going on. What are you up to?"

"Getting ready to take care of some firewood. Feel free to come help...it would make it easier on my old bones," I say, just joking around.

"Actually, that sounds good. I need to do something and I'd rather come hang out with you than sit here by myself. Be there soon."

Sure as shit, Drew pulls up in the driveway a little while later. He climbs out of his truck and I notice he's clean-shaven and looks like he got a haircut. He's a good-looking guy. I'm not sure why he's single.

"Hey Drew, nice haircut. I was kidding about you coming over to help," I tell him.

He smiles at me, and says, "I know, but I needed something to do. My mind is wandering."

"Well, hard work'll take care of that." I hand him an axe and we get to work.

He helps me cut and stack firewood and then we change the oil in my truck. We talk and joke around while we work, which makes the day go by quickly. We work effortlessly together, like we can read each other's mind. Every now and then, I feel the little hairs on the back of my neck stand up and I look up to find Drew looking at me. He immediately glances away, and I'm not sure what to think of it.

Around noon, we grab some lunch from the kitchen. Grady stops by and joins us for lunch. I barely ever see the kid anymore.

"Hey Grady, did you get off work early today? How's the apartment search going?" I ask.

"Yep. I've got my yearly physical this afternoon. Headed there next. The apartment hunt is going okay. I've looked at a couple of places, but the rent is high. I filled out an application for one apartment over on Main Street, above one of the restaurants. If they approve me, I might be moving there soon."

"Wow! That's great for you. Still close to home and not a bad drive to work every day. Looks like we'll have an empty bedroom then."

"Yeah," Grady says. "Maybe Drew can rent the room from you since he's homeless, and he's always here anyway," he says jokingly.

"I'm happy being homeless!" Drew laughs. "I save a lot of money that way."

"How's your girlfriend doing?" I ask.

"Charlotte is doing fine. She's looking forward to some time off from college between semesters in January. We're talking about her moving in to the apartment when I move. She's away at college most of the year anyway, so she'd only be there on her breaks." He looks at me, almost as if to see how I'll react to that bombshell.

"Well, you guys are technically adults now, so if that's what you want to do, I wish you the best of luck. Just be careful how you go about certain things, if you know what I mean." I raise my eyebrows at him in expectation.

"Yes, Dad, I know what you mean," he says, rolling his eyes. "Don't worry. We'll be safe. I'm not ready to be a dad yet. She hasn't mentioned it to her parents, but I'm not so sure they will accept it as easily as you. They're having a formal fundraising gala on Saturday and she's hoping to mention it to them there. We want our parents to be okay with our choices, but I'm not so sure it'll go over too well with them."

After some catching up for a few minutes, Grady says, "I've got to get to my appointment. Good to see you guys. Thanks for the sandwich!"

Drew and I finish our lunch and clean up. I throw a load of laundry into the washer to get that big chore started. The firewood and oil change went faster than normal since Drew was here to help, so I might see what else we can get done today if he doesn't mind helping. Emerson works so hard at work, then has to come home to take care of whatever I can't get to around the house. Plus, she has to take care of the kids and Declan is a handful.

"Hey, Drew? You feeling homemaker-ish? I was thinking about doing some cooking to help out with dinners for Emerson when she's alone with the kids. Feel like helping? The two of us could knock it out in no time, and it would really help Emerson in the evenings when I'm not here."

"Sure. What are we making?" Drew is happy to help cook some make-ahead meals for the family. We cook several family-sized portions of chicken noodle soup, chicken pot pie, macaroni and cheese, and cheesy potato casserole to package and freeze. These will come in handy to help out with dinner on the nights I'm at work. We keep one chicken pot pie dish out to have for dinner tonight.

"You should stay for dinner tonight since you helped cook it," I mention.

"Sounds good to me. The alternative is fast food on the way back to the station." Drew tries to eat healthy, but it's not always easy when you're a firefighter. Throw in his lack of a permanent home to go to, and it makes it even more difficult.

Drew

I'll never pass up a good home-cooked meal and I never mind working for it. I'm actually glad I can help. It gives me something to do and makes me feel like I'm needed. I'm sure it's tough taking care of a family when one parent works shift work and the other has a full-time job.

Keegan gets off the bus around 3:00pm, says hello, and takes her backpack to her bedroom to start on her homework. Around 4:00pm, Declan bursts through the door with a ton of energy, drops his stuff at the front door, and goes straight for the kitchen to find a snack.

"Declan, please put your things where they go. They don't go in front of the door. Get started on your homework while I cook dinner." Owen sighs.

"Ugh. Dad, why? I don't want to do homework. Why do we have homework when we've been in school for seven hours already today?" Declan whines.

"I am not having this conversation with you, Declan," he says sternly. Declan continues grumbling as he heads to the table to do his homework. It's difficult for him to focus, so he needs someone around to help him get it done. I decide to sit down to help him and, together, we get it done in no time.

Emerson comes home around 5:00pm and looks exhausted. Owen hugs her and asks, "How was your day?"

"It would have been okay if the principal didn't come observe my lesson right after recess when the kids were so full of energy that they couldn't sit still. And on the same day that two different students threw up on the classroom floor. I'm exhausted." She puts her purse and teacher bag down and heads to the kitchen. "What's that I smell?"

Owen massages her shoulders with his strong hands while he says, "Drew and I went ahead and took care of dinner for tonight, so you sit and rest your feet. I know walking on that hard floor all day strains your back. We also cooked extra meals to freeze as make-ahead meals for the busy nights. All you have to do is thaw them and pop them in the oven."

Emerson's eyes tear up. "Are you serious? That is incredible!"

"If it's a good thing, why are you crying, Honey?" Owen asks.

"Because it is such a relief to have the extra help. I just feel like I have so much going on that having a little help around here is just...I really appreciate it. Thank you."

"Drew helped, too. We tackled it together, along with the firewood and a few other things."

She comes to hug me. "Thank you for helping, Drew. I might have to get you to come around more often!" she says with a laugh.

"I'm happy to help," I tell her. I really am. Owen is my best friend and his family is like family to me. Owen and I talk about yesterday's football game while we work on cleaning up the kitchen from the cooking we did today.

"You've got more work to do?" I ask when I go back to the living room and see that Emerson is grading papers.

"Yeah, unfortunately. There's no time during the school day to get these graded, so I have to do it at home."

"That doesn't seem fair. You're working on your own time." I tell her. "Can I do anything to help?"

"No, you've already helped enough. I can get this done. Thank you, though." She gives me a smile and continues to mark the papers one by one until they are all graded and the kids have made their way to the living room to watch TV. When Emerson's done grading, we all sit together and enjoy the chicken pot pie Owen and I made for dinner. Emerson insists on cleaning up after we eat dinner, since we cooked so much today, and then we all relax and watch a show together until it's time for the kids to go to bed.

I head back to the station for the night, shower, and daydream about hanging out, enjoying a meal, and watching TV with a family of my own.

CHAPTER 11

Emerson

IT'S SUNDAY, SO I'M doing my lesson plans for the week. I've been working on them for a few hours and I really feel like I need to get out of the house. I haven't seen Owen in two days, so I decide to stop by the station to say hi and take him and the guys some of their favorite donuts from Duck Donuts. It's always like Christmas when you get to enjoy one of those warm, delicious orbs of goodness.

I texted Owen to let him know I was coming, but I didn't hear anything back, which means they're probably out on a call. Pulling up to the Riverfront Fire Station, I realize all the bay doors are open and two trucks are gone. I head inside where the only sounds are the whoosh and clunk of the air compressor the remaining firetruck is plugged into. Setting the donuts down on the counter in the kitchen, I'm startled when Drew walks in.

"Hey Em, what are you doing here?" He saunters over to hug me. "Where are the kids?"

"I thought I'd bring you guys a treat. I had to get out of the house. I felt cooped up. The kids are at home. When I left, Keegan was on the phone and Declan was practicing his soccer moves out back. They didn't want to come with me. Where's everyone at?"

"They had a call back out to that marshy area along the York River that keeps flaring up. They only needed two trucks today. This is the fifth time we've been called out to the same area," he explains. He looks tired, as though he's been run ragged without a break.

"Really? I'm sorry to hear that. I'm glad you got to sit this one out, though. You look exhausted."

"I guess I am," he sighs as his shoulders deflate. "We've been going constantly. A few days ago, the brush fire was so big they had to call in assistance from neighboring counties and volunteer stations. I don't think the fires are accidents. This many fires in the same area can't be. The fire inspector is investigating it with the state police. They found the point of origin when they got on scene today.

"From what I heard over the radio, it sounds like someone used gasoline to torch some trees. The trees were charred from trunk to leaves, and the fire spread from there because the gasoline was poured along the ground like someone walked away with the gas container upside down, trying to get every last drop out."

"Oh, wow! I just don't understand why someone would start fires intentionally. I hadn't heard that. Of course, I've barely seen Owen. I think I see you just as much as I see him. Any idea when they'll be back?" I ask.

"Arsonists are usually bored, vengeful, or psychotic," he says, shaking his head. "I just heard the trucks report that the fire is contained, so hopefully it won't take long for them to get it completely out. Then they'll clean up and head back to the station. Do you want to hang out until they get here?"

"Sure, that'd be great. I'm not ready to head back home yet. What were you doing when I got here?"

"Working around the station until about 4:00pm. I worked out in the gym for an hour, then washed a couple of the trucks and did some of my training. Now, I'm just hanging out in the day room watching TV."

Drew leads me to the dayroom and we sit on the couch, watching the evening news. We're the only two people downstairs in the dayroom. Firefighter Muller is upstairs in his bunk, and Stathes is out in the bay washing the ambulance, but neither of them comes inside.

"And this just in," the news reporter says sternly, "Local law enforcement has found evidence of arson in the recent brush fires along the river. The state fire investigator says accelerants have been found in generic household containers left behind at the point of origin. In addition to fingerprint examination, further analysis of the liquids and their containers is ongoing. And now, here's Jake with the weather..."

***

IN THE DARKNESS, I hear the news anchors signing off and announcing Jeopardy coming up next. My eyelids flutter open and I realize my head is on Drew's shoulder.

"Oh my goodness! I must've fallen asleep...and on your shoulder, too. I'm so sorry!" As I feel the heat rising in my face, I wipe my sleepy eyes, knowing I'm blushing.

"It's okay, that's what friends are for," Drew reassures me, his comforting voice easing my worries. He yawns and stretches like a tiger just rousing from an afternoon nap in the sun. "I think I dozed off, too, actually. You're tired. I take it as a compliment that you're comfortable enough around me to fall asleep. I'm sorry you're so exhausted." He reaches up to put a loose strand of hair behind my ear, smiling that gorgeous dimpled smile of his, and I find myself relaxing back into the couch.

"Drew, you're so easy to be around. I never feel like we have to make idle conversation like I do around some people. I'm always comfortable around you," I tell him truthfully.

When Jeopardy comes on, I ask him, "How about one of those donuts?" He nods, so we both walk to the kitchen.

"What's your favorite kind?" he asks me, grabbing a napkin for each of us.

"I love the cinnamon roll donuts. How about you?"

"The cookies and cream donuts have to be my favorite," he answers.

"That's Owen's favorite kind, too."

We both reach for our cherished confectionary sweet and dive in, standing right at the counter in front of the box, moaning at the delectable taste. I can feel Drew's moan travel through my body like a rumble of thunder during a summer storm. Each sultry groan sends a shiver straight to my core. I have to try hard to either ignore him or hide my reaction to him.

Before I realize what's happened, a smirk appears on his face, along with that damn irresistible dimple.

"You've got something..." He points back and forth from his face to my face. He finally just reaches over to my face and uses his finger to gently swipe glaze from the side of my mouth and puts his finger in front of my lips so I can lick the glaze off. I can't help but suck the syrupy sweetness from his skin. Our eyes lock on each other's and I can't look away.

I feel like I'm on fire, burning from the inside out. He slowly pulls his finger from my lips and steadily eases closer to me until there's only an inch between us. I can feel the heat emanating from his body to mine. He looks down at me and, if I didn't know any better, I'd swear he wants to kiss me. He glances from my eyes to my lips. He licks his lips and I find myself inadvertently mirroring him. His tempting blue eyes gaze into mine. His body is so close, I can just barely feel his arousal growing by the second.

"Emerson, you are so beautiful. I haven't been this attracted to a woman since my wife," he says so softly I can barely hear him.

"Drew, I'm..."

"Married, I know," he continues in a hushed voice. I barely notice him place his hand on my neck, caressing my cheek with his thumb. "Owen's one lucky man. I know I shouldn't be thinking about you the way I do, but I can't help it. You are absolutely the perfect woman in every way. I wish..." His quiet voice trails off as though he's not sure he should continue.

"You wish what?" I urge him on. Nothing can happen, but I want to know what's going through his mind.

"I wish you weren't married or..." He closes his eyes momentarily and shakes his head like he's trying to clear it. Opening his gorgeous eyes, he says, "I wish I could share you with Owen," he utters impulsively. His hand drops and he immediately backs away from me with wide eyes, covering his mouth with his hand.

"Oh, shit! I am so sorry, Emerson. I should not have said that. It was extremely inappropriate of me. I'm just so comfortable with you. I feel like I could tell you anything. Please forget I said that." His face is turning different shades of red as he backs away from me even further, as though I'm poisonous.

I hold my hands up like I'm surrendering, as though I need to show that I have no ill intent. "It's okay, Drew. There's nothing to worry about. It was just me and you, and you were just thinking out loud. I'm sure we both just got caught up in the moment. We can forget it." I smile at him to show I mean it and he seems to relax a little.

He takes a deep breath and slowly exhales. "Okay. I think I'm going to head up to my bunk room now. I'm sure I have some online training to do." He walks—almost runs—toward the stairs and it's the last I see of him. It's probably a good thing because...damn! What he said! Never in a million years would I have said something like that out loud—sharing myself with two men has only recently become a fantasy in my daydreams.

I have to admit, though, my initial bodily response was heat, interest, arousal, and excitement, before my brain ruefully shut it all down.

***

Drew

WHAT THE FUCK WAS I thinking?!

I mean... What. The. Actual. Fuck?!

I crash into my bed and cover my face with my arms. I can't believe I said that out loud to her. I'm such a fucking dumbass. Now I'm at risk of losing my best friend—well, two best friends, if I'm honest. If Owen finds out I said that, he'll hate me. He'll never speak to me again.

She's right. We both just got caught up in the moment.

Wait a minute.

Both. She said we *both* got caught up in the moment.

Does that mean...?

CHAPTER 12

Owen

I JUMP OFF THE truck and immediately take off my turnout gear to hang it up. We were at that call for hours on end, and hot spots kept flaring back up when we thought it was contained, but we eventually doused the fire for good. I hope the fire inspector can figure out who's behind this. There is no way all these fires are accidents. What scares me is that each time it restarts, it gets closer and closer to people's homes. That's when this pyromaniac could become a murderer.

I'm walking through the kitchen when I see my favorite snack—Duck Donuts—and a note.

> *Owen,*
> *Stopped by to see you and brought some treats for you and the guys. I stayed for a while, but figured I'd head back home and get some grading done. I'll see you when you get home. Be safe.*
>
> *I love you,*
> *Emerson*

Best. Wife. Ever. I honestly don't know how she puts up with the fire life, but I'm thankful for her. I grab a donut and head upstairs to wash the soot and sweat off of me from the last call. I've got a three day break—it's my Kelly Day—starting tomorrow and I can't wait to get home to Emerson and the kids and get some time away from this station. I don't know who Kelly is, but I'm thankful as fuck that we get an extra day off now and then because of them.

***

WALKING IN THE FRONT door at home the next morning is relaxing. It's like the weight of my job rolls off my shoulders just by walking through the doorway. I've got a list a mile long of things I need to take care of since I've been working nonstop lately.

I grab some breakfast and get started on my list so I can finish before Emerson and the kids get home from school.

The first thing I do is get some vegetable beef stew going in the crock pot for dinner tonight, so Emerson won't have to cook. I get some laundry done so we don't get behind on that and then head outside to take care of the yard.

The kids get off the bus and do their usual thing. Emerson doesn't get home until about 5:00pm. While we're eating dinner, we talk about our day, what's been going on at work and school, and generally catch up since I've been gone for three days. As usual, Declan complains that he doesn't like what we've cooked and I tell him to either eat it or make himself something else. I'm not making a different meal for each person. He gets up and makes himself a sandwich, with a side of drama and whining.

After dinner, we all take our showers, get ready for bed, and relax with some TV. Emerson's lounging beside me on the couch, leaning into me with her hand resting on my chest and I'm holding her with my arm around her waist. I'm really lucky to have my family. Life gets stressful sometimes with my schedule, and I can't wait until I can retire, so that stress goes away, but I love our life.

"I hate to be the bearer of bad news, guys, but it's bedtime. You've got school tomorrow," I tell the kids.

Keegan and Declan say goodnight and head to bed and then Emerson turns to me, saying, "Owen, I want to talk to you about something."

"Sure, of course. Let's get comfortable in bed and we'll talk." We lock up the house and when we're comfortable in bed, I give her my attention rather than turning the TV on.

"What's on your mind?"

"You know yesterday when I stopped by the station? I talked with Drew while I was waiting for you to get back from that fire call. We watched some TV in the day-room and we were both so tired we fell asleep on the couch."

"Yeah, I'm sorry I wasn't there. That call took a while to finish up. I saw your note. It was really nice of you to bring us donuts. The guys loved them." I kiss her nose.

"The thing is," she begins. She seems nervous to talk to me about whatever's on her mind. "When Drew and I ate donuts, I got a little glaze on my mouth, and Drew wiped it off. I'm sure it was innocent. He put his finger up to my mouth for me to lick the glaze off. You know, like you would do if you were helping a toddler eat. But then there was this, I don't know, moment, I guess. We looked at each other. Drew started talking to me and said he thought I was beautiful."

"He's always said that. So what's the big deal?"

"He mentioned that he thought I was the perfect woman and that he wished I wasn't married," she says. Now I'm getting worried.

"Well, that's too bad. You are married. You're mine. He can deal with it."

"Then, he impulsively blurted out that he would share me with you if he could," she says cautiously.

By now, my blood pressure is through the roof, and I need to punch something.

Emerson puts her hand on my arm, probably to calm me, and continues, "But he felt bad right away. He realized what he said and immediately apologized, saying that was inappropriate and he didn't mean to say it. He asked me to please forget he said anything, and I agreed. I feel like I need to tell you because I don't want to hide anything from you. I want to be honest with you. Nothing happened, but

I just wanted you to know about our conversation. Please don't be mad."

"I'm not mad at you. I'm mad at him! What kind of fucking friend says that to my wife? He knows we're married. He's always said you were attractive, but I never thought he'd act on it." I get up and grab my keys. "I'm going to kick his ass!"

"Please don't, Owen," Emerson says, pulling me back to the bed. "He regretted saying it immediately. It must have been something he thought about and accidentally said it out loud. Please don't let your friendship end over this. The only reason I'm saying anything is I don't want to feel like I'm hiding anything from you."

Sucking in a deep breath, I say, "He shouldn't be thinking things like that. What did you say back to him?" I'm glad my wife is being honest with me, but this is killing me.

"I just told him that we could forget it happened. We both just got caught up in the moment."

"What moment? Did something else happen?"

"No, Honey. We just talked, but I felt like you should know about a conversation like that. It's not something someone tells you every day. It's been on my mind a lot since then, and it was, well, thought-provoking."

"Are you saying you were interested in what he was saying? Do you wish you were single?" I'm afraid of her answer. Firefighters have a high divorce rate because of the demands of their jobs. It's a dangerous career. I'm barely ever home. We don't get to talk, or do other things, as much as a regular married couple might. I'm constantly trying to make up for being gone when I do come home. Hearing her tell me this is the end would be the worst thing I've ever heard in my life. I feel like this might be the beginning of my world crashing down around me.

"No! Not at all. There was just a moment when we looked at each other and, to be honest, I think we were attracted to each other. It wasn't just on his side. I would never cheat on you, Owen. He is a handsome, intelligent man, though. I'm not going to lie and say I don't find him attractive. Then again, he did say it was an accident to begin with, anyway. He may have accidentally said something about sharing me, but that doesn't mean he actually wants to do it. There's a big difference between fantasy and reality," Emerson says quietly.

It doesn't surprise me that she thinks he's handsome. Women hit on him every time we're out in public together. He's even had a couple of guys hit on him.

"I can see why you'd think he's handsome, but I think it would hurt less if you'd just lie to me. Are you telling me you don't love me anymore? Is this your way of telling me you want a divorce?" I can hear the crevice in my heart cracking open wider with each word I speak.

Emerson throws her arms around my neck, saying, "God, no! I want you forever, Owen. I love you with all of my heart."

"I love you too, Baby, and I don't want to share you with anyone. I almost wish you hadn't told me anything."

"That wouldn't be honest. We can't help who we're attracted to. It just happens." She lowers her voice. "If I'm honest, when he said he wanted to share me with you..." She hesitates for a moment, then looks into my eyes and continues, "It kind of turned me on. I found it intriguing. The initial reaction my body had was surprising, and then my brain shut it all down right away, because of course, we're married. I've thought about it a lot, though. There are people in the world who have relationships with more than two people in them." She waits, judging my reaction. "Have you ever considered it?"

"No, and I'm not going to consider it now. You're mine." With my hand behind her neck, I pull her to me and take her lips in a possessive kiss like the neanderthal I am so I can prove to her that she's mine. I'm not sharing her with anyone. Ever.

I pull her shirt up and over her head, and she gasps when I ravage her breasts. I suck, lick, and gently bite until there are sure to be marks on her skin tomorrow to prove that she's mine. I kiss my way down her chest and stomach to her waist, then remove her sleep shorts so I can suck on the flesh at the apex of her thigh. She's mine and I will mark her. I move to bite and suck her other thigh, massaging her hips as I go. It isn't until she's moaning out loud that I finally make my way to her pussy. She's already soaking wet. *Is that from me or from the conversation we were having?*

Emerson has her hands on my head and she's spreading her legs wide open to give me all the access I want. Her passionate sighs urge me on and make me want to give her the best orgasm of her life. *I'm not sharing her.*

Chapter 13

OWEN HAS NEVER BEEN this possessive before. He is encompassing me with his entire body. His mouth and hands are all over me. I grasp his head between my legs as he licks between my folds and sucks my clit. Then he picks his head up, stares into my eyes, and slides his two middle fingers inside of me, pumping them in and out with abandon. He rubs my clit with his thumb at the same time and, at this rate, it won't take long for me to come. I think he can see it in my face and he moves up my body while taking off his shorts.

When he's hovering over me, face to face, he growls, "You. Are. MINE." Then he positions himself at my entrance and thrusts himself into me harder than he ever has before. It feels so good that I don't ever want it to end.

"Harder," I beg. "You feel so fucking good." He increases his speed and intensity until we're both panting with sweat beading on our foreheads.

"God, Emerson, you're squeezing me tight. I can feel your pussy clenching around me." His dirty words knock me over the edge and I come harder than I ever have in my life.

"Owen, you're incredible. Let me feel you come inside of me." He lets go with a sultry groan and fills me up. We lay there in serenity, enjoying the perfect fit of our bodies, until we start drifting off. Then Owen grabs a washcloth from the bathroom to clean us up and climbs into bed next to me, wraps his arms around me, and we fall asleep together.

***

WHEN I WAKE IN the morning, he's looking at me with a strange look on his face. I raise an eyebrow as if to ask why he's looking at me.

"I don't want to lose you, Emerson," he admits.

"Owen, you will never lose me. I promise. Are we okay?"

"Yeah, Babe, we're okay. I love you."

"I love you, too, Honey. Always."

We hug and he kisses me tenderly. Unfortunately, it's time for me to get ready for work and then get the kids up and off to school. Organized chaos ensues as we're all running around grabbing breakfast, getting our stuff, and heading out the door. Before I leave, I turn to Owen for one more hug and kiss.

"Have a good day, Honey," I say. "Do you think you'll talk to Drew today?"

"Yeah, he's supposed to come over today. I promise I'll try not to kill him, but I'm still pissed at him," he says.

"Don't hurt your best friend, Honey." Kiss. "I love you."

"I love you, too."

Drew

Emerson

Hi Drew. I wanted to let you know I talked to Owen last night and he knows about our conversation. I had to be honest with him, otherwise I would feel like I'm hiding something from him.

Drew

I completely understand, Em. Thanks for letting me know. Should I wear a bullet proof vest when I head to the house today? :)

Emerson

I don't think you'll need one, but he is upset.

Me and my goddamn big fucking mouth. I can't help that I think of Emerson so much. I think of her as a best friend, just like Owen. I can't get her out of my head. I don't know what I was thinking when I blurted out that I'd be willing to share her with Owen. He'd have to be willing, too, and I'm sure he is not about to even consider it.

Emerson thinks I'm a good man? She probably wouldn't think that if she knew what kind of thoughts possess my mind. She'd think differently about me if she knew I daydream about her sinuous body in every erotic position I can think of while her husband watches us.

The drive over to Owen's house is a long one today. I know Emerson and the kids will be at school, so it'll just be me and him. No one to save my ass if he decides to beat the shit out of me. I pull up the driveway and notice he's already outside working in the yard. I could use some strenuous work, too, so I get out of the truck and head that way.

"Hey man. Can I help?" I ask hesitantly, as I walk up to Owen. He's clearly been out here working out some anger issues for at least a couple of hours already.

"What the fuck, man? I thought we were friends. And now this? You hit on my wife?" Owen is so angry that his face is red. "I had calmed myself down until I saw you pull up the driveway. Just seeing you pisses me off. How does a good friend like you go and make a move on my wife behind my back?" Just as he says the words 'behind my back,' he draws his fist back and slams it into my face, drawing a stream of blood from my nose.

My eyes squeeze shut in pain and both hands fly up to my nose as blood drips down my shirt.

"Ow, fuck! Owen, it wasn't like that. It just happened. I opened my big mouth and spewed my guts to her. I didn't mean to. And nothing happened. I just talked to her." I dare to open my eyes and look at his hurt expression, still holding my nose, so that maybe it'll stop bleeding.

"How do you tell your best friend's wife that you want her? Who does that? How do you even sleep at night?" He's screaming at me as he throws another punch.

"It was an accident," I grind out. With no air in my lungs, it's hard to talk. "I didn't mean to say it. It just came out. The more time I spend around you and your family, the more comfortable I get. It was just me and her at the station. I don't know what I was thinking. I wasn't thinking, I guess," I try to explain.

"No, you clearly weren't thinking. So is it true? Do you actually want to be with Emerson? Tell me it's just a fantasy you don't actually plan to act out." Owen stares at me with expectation. *Do I tell him the truth?*

"Owen, I don't know how to answer that," I say honestly. He must not like that answer because he gives me a right hook to my kidney. I just stand there and take it because this is all my fault and I'm not going to hit my best friend.

"Hit me back, asshole!" he yells. "There's gonna be a fight today. You can't mess with Emerson and get away with it. I'm not going to let you end my marriage. She's MY wife. I will not let her go." Owen hits me again, right in my left eye. I'm thrown backwards, but I right myself and then I stand my ground.

"I'm not gonna hit you back, man. You have every right to kick my ass. Go ahead. I deserve it. Hold me accountable for my dumbass big mouth. I'm sorry I messed things up. I shouldn't have said anything at all to her, but if I'm honest, I can't help how I feel...about her...and you." Owen slams his fist into my stomach once more for good measure. Then he backs off as I'm dry heaving and clutching my stomach. We're both bent over and gasping for air.

"Are you surprised I have feelings for her? I constantly tell you how lucky you are to have her and how hot she is. We all spend all of our time together. We've all become best friends. She's perfect, and you know it." I hope I'm helping him understand where I'm coming from, but at the very least, I hope I'm convincing him to stop hitting me. It would benefit him to slow down on the punches, considering his torn-up, bloody knuckles.

I inhale strength and exhale frustration, saying, "Think about it, man. Have you even considered it? We'd all have someone there for us all the time. You'd have someone else around the house to help take care of your family. The kids would have more support and attention.

"Life is hard working shift work like we do, especially with all the overtime we have to work. Wouldn't it make sense to have someone else around that can improve life for all of us? You, Emerson, and your family are the only people I have. Let me be there for you, too. Just think about it."

And it looks like he is actually thinking about it. He's standing there with his feet planted like a mountain, fists clenched beside his thighs, trying to compose himself, but staring at me in distress and despair.

"What would people think? How would it even work?" Owen says.

"Who gives a shit what other people think? I don't. You shouldn't either. I've already lost one love of my life and my son. I'm not about to let society or people I don't fucking know or respect tell me what to do with my life. We get to decide how it will work. All I'm saying is consider your life and how it could be different; how it could be better. I'm willing to take a chance on you and Emerson."

"You want me to take a chance on losing my family?" he asks incredulously.

"I want you to take a chance on me. Give me a chance. Give us a chance."

"What if it doesn't work? This isn't some fucking movie, Drew, where everyone gets what they want and lives happily ever after. It's real life."

"We can have what we want, but we have to be willing to take the chance, Owen. I'm not trying to take Emerson away from you. I'm trying to tell you I'd like to be a part of your relationship with her; with both of you. I'm not taking anything away, but adding something of value, hopefully. Consider whether Emerson is even interested in being with two men. Just keep an open mind."

This is not what I expected to say when I came over today. I had planned on apologizing, taking a few punches, and then, hopefully, moving past it and, at the very least, remaining friends with Owen. Something is making me dig in my heels and try to get through to him.

"And what if I agreed to something like this? What then? Does that make me gay?" Owen's face flushes red.

"No, not necessarily, but we can explore that thought. Are you attracted to men?"

"No."

"Are you attracted to me?" I venture.

"I've never really thought about it. Since I met you, you've always been there for me. You're my best friend. Drew, you're like a brother to me. I mean, I guess I can see why women would find you attractive. I don't want to lose you as a friend."

That wasn't a 'no.' I take a step closer to him and look him in the eyes, trying to feel whatever it is that he can't find the words to say.

"Owen, I'm baring my soul to you. I'm laying it all on the line here. I'm not saying I want a relationship with just Emerson. I'm interested in being in a triad relationship with both of you. It would only be the three of us; no one else. Owen, you're more than a brother to me. Will you please take some time to think about it?

"I wish we could all sit and talk about what we might want or be interested in exploring. We can figure it out as we go if you and Emerson are willing. Your family has become my family. I'd do anything for you, Emerson, and the kids. Look, if you have questions or want to keep talking about it, let's talk. If not, let's get this yard cleaned up and offload some of this anxious energy we both seem to have."

"No." Owen mutters quietly, stepping back. "No, I think you should go."

CHAPTER 14

I'VE WORKED FOR HOURS out in the yard. It's probably a good thing I'm doing so much manual labor today, because otherwise I probably would've beaten Drew to a pulp. I was so angry when Emerson told me what he said. Then, that night, I became this selfish, greedy animal and had to mark my territory. Emerson seemed to like it, though, thank fuck.

Drew isn't wrong. He definitely gave me something to think about. Living the fire life is hard and it would make sense to have another adult around. Someone else to talk to; depend on. Someone else to help with the kids and help around the house.

Hell, Drew's already been doing that, but now he wants to *help* with Emerson, too. My first thoughts were *hell no*, but should I discuss this with Emerson to see if it's actually what she wants? I know it's what Drew wants. Is it fair to

Emerson to not hear her out? Not listen to her feelings and desires?

These thoughts are circling my head all day as I work in the yard. I can't believe Drew was willing to stick around after I beat the shit out of him. He really is a good guy. His nose finally stopped bleeding before he left, but his eye had already started turning black and blue. I made him leave because I didn't know how to act around him or what to say. I feel like I'm losing my wife and my best friend all at once. I need time to think. I need time to talk to Emerson about all this.

Emerson

On the drive home from work this afternoon, I have no idea what to expect when I walk through the door. I know Drew was hanging out with Owen today.

Is everything okay? Did Owen tear him limb from limb? Do I need to go bail Owen out of jail?

I park my car in the driveway and note that Drew is not here. I head inside, put my bags down, and find Owen sitting in front of the TV. He's already had his shower; I can tell by his freshly shaved head and face.

"The yard looks great, Honey. You did a lot of work today," I say.

"Thanks."

"Is everything okay with you and Drew?" I wonder aloud.

He sighs heavily. "I don't know, Emerson. I guess we need to talk about some things."

I give him a hug and tell him I'm happy to talk about anything he wants. "Let's have dinner and then we can talk."

We manage to work together to make spaghetti, a salad, and garlic bread, but it's a quiet process. He won't look at me and he doesn't touch me even once. We just meander around the kitchen in silence, tension hanging in the air at the thought of the conversation to come. We have a very quiet dinner together with the kids and then the kids go off to play outside. The weather is getting warmer, so they're taking advantage of that.

Owen and I sit on the back deck with drinks in hand and try to relax, but there is a negative charge in the air that I can't shake.

"Owen, let's talk. Please. What did you and Drew talk about today? What happened?"

After a long moment, as though he's contemplating telling me or not, he says, "Drew apologized for what he said to you. He's not sorry about what he said, because he meant it. He's just sorry that he accidentally let it slip and might have ruined our relationships. And he stood there and took every punch I threw without hitting me back. Refused to. He said he deserved it."

My heart is breaking for these two men. "Oh, Owen. What else happened? Are you still friends?"

"I don't know. I guess. I made him leave because I just didn't know how to talk to him or what to say. He's like a brother to me. I've never considered being in a relationship with three people. It's not how I was raised. It's not the norm. All kinds of thoughts have been running through my head since you told me."

"Like what?" I ask him. "What are you thinking? Talk to me."

"If we do this, does it mean I'm bisexual? What will everyone think?"

"Owen, we can't let what someone else will think stop us from being happy. It doesn't matter that you weren't raised in a polyamorous relationship. I wasn't either. But, if I'm honest, I'm interested in at least discussing it. I care a great deal for Drew and I know you do, too. He's become a part of our family. How do you feel about him?"

"I'm not sure. I can't fathom losing him as a friend and not having him in my life anymore. I've never thought about kissing him or anything."

"You don't have to. We can talk to Drew and find out what each of us is comfortable with. There are many ways this could work. I think it could be good for all of us to sit together and get everything out in the open. At the very least, we can find a way to continue being friends."

"I know. I just...don't know. You know?" A nervous laugh escapes him. "Drew said the same thing. He has become like family to us. He's alone in the world. I can't imagine what that's like. No place to call home. Drew said it would be helpful to have another adult around to help with the kids. He's not wrong. Can we just take some time to think more about it?" he pleads.

I walk over to his chair and pull him up by the hand. "Of course, Honey. I don't want to do anything you're not comfortable with. I don't want to lose you." I wrap my arms around him to convey just how much I truly care about him. We watch the sunset from the deck and then head inside to wind down for the day and start fresh tomorrow.

Drew

I've been at the station all day, every day, and I need to get out of here. I never intended for this to happen. I haven't been to the Callaghan's house or talked to my two best friends in over a week, and I am absolutely empty inside.

There was such an immense weight lifted off my shoulders when I told Emerson how I felt, though. Then talking to Owen and being honest about it all was a tremendous relief, too. A painful one, but a relief nonetheless. I've always thought Emerson was exquisite since the day I first laid eyes on her. Owen and I clicked right away and became friends on my first day on the job. If someone had told me then that I would fall for them, I'd have told them they're crazy, but now? Things have changed. We've spent so much time together and gotten to know one another. The more I know about them, their kids, their life, the more I crave to be a part of it.

Owen was right. At first, it was just a fantasy about two of my close friends; an erotic notion I'd think about when I would daydream or when I'd fall asleep at night. I'd imagine Owen telling me that I could have my turn with Emerson tonight, or that I could join them in their bedroom. I'd pretend Owen wanted to watch me please Emerson until all three of us would come together. Then I started thinking about holding both of them as we would fall asleep together.

The more I thought about it, the more real it became. I started thinking about what it would be like to hold Emerson's and Owen's hands walking on the beach at sunset.

Then my thoughts evolved to picturing how it would feel to come home to my family at the end of my shift and spend time together watching TV at night before bed. I pictured home-cooked meals together at the dining table, mowing the lawn, fixing things around the house, and protecting the ones I love. And it was always Emerson, Owen, and their sweet kids. Not once did I envision anyone else in these daydreams.

Finally, I started hoping that maybe this was something that might actually work. I realized the benefits of this kind of relationship. All I can do is hope that, in time, Emerson and Owen will either keep open minds and we can talk about the possibilities, or that we can at least remain friends. The alternative is too devastating to consider.

Owen

It's been a few days since the last conversation Emerson and I had about exploring a polyamorous relationship with Drew. We've spoken a few times about it, trying to get all our thoughts, wishes, and fears out in the open. I've done nothing but think about it. They make some good points. It's just never been an option to me. It wasn't something I even considered. Now that the idea is in my head, it's thought-provoking. Drew has sparked a desire in me I never knew could exist.

I'm trying to focus on my station chores and the training I need to do, but my head is not in the game today. I've thought of so many questions that I've decided that the three of us just need to get together and talk about what we want. That's the only way to answer the questions and move forward.

I cannot lose my wife. I don't want to lose my best friend. We've got the kids to think about, too. It's all too much, so I text Emerson and Drew to try to put my mind—and hopefully theirs, too—at ease.

Owen

> I'm miserable. Can we find a time to get together and talk about things? I think that's the only way we can move forward.

I continue washing the truck and scrub the wheels harder than I should because of everything going on in my head. Finally, my phone dings.

Emerson

> Of course. How about we see if the kids want to spend the night at your parents' house on Saturday and talk at our house?

That's fine with me, but I'm going to wait to see what Drew says.

Drew

> Definitely. I'll be there. Just let me know what time.

We finish texting about what time Drew should come over and then I get back to washing the truck. Terrance walks through the bay and mentions, "Wow, man. That's the cleanest I've ever seen the brush truck. If you keep going, though, you're gonna end up scraping off the paint." He walks out of the bay howling like a fucking hyena because he thinks he's hilarious.

"Shut up, asswipe," I call after him. I think everyone in the station knows something's up. I'm not usually this rude with people and the guys have given me a wide berth at work. They're all pretty much staying away from me unless it's absolutely necessary that they talk to me. I can't blame them. This whole situation has got me nauseous and acting like a jerk. Hopefully, we'll get things cleared up Saturday.

CHAPTER 15

Emerson

IT'S BEEN A ROUGH couple of weeks. I'm glad February is a short month. I'm trying to continue my lessons at school, but all I can think about is Owen and Drew and whether we're all falling apart or coming together. We're supposed to get together to talk this weekend.

On top of that, I've got the kids to worry about.

Grady is moving into an apartment he was approved for on Main Street. It's still close to us, so we'll still see him. He's been packing boxes and moving his things over to his new place. He's so excited to start adulting and here I am drowning in adulthood.

Keegan is upset about her boyfriend at school, and I've tried my best to help her through that. It's making her grades fall. She's a smart girl, but she's so worried about what this guy thinks of her that she's not doing all her work. Zeroes bring your grades down fast.

To top it all off, Declan's teacher called me today at work and said he has been disrupting class with crazy outbursts, throwing things across the room, and talking to other students during work time and even while taking tests. I promised her I'd speak to Declan and we'd find a way to discipline him tonight.

The bell rings letting us know it's time for lunch and I head to the teachers' lounge on the other side of the building. I don't know why they call it a lounge. It's not like anyone relaxes in there. The chairs aren't even comfortable. We pop in and eat for five minutes, then have to make copies, talk to the principal, meet with a parent, or something else that takes away from our lunch time.

I see Lauren eating already and set my lunch beside her. I'm a little more winded from the long walk than I usually am.

"How's everything going, Emerson?" she says.

"You want the honest truth or the regular platitudes?" I ask. Just then, I start to feel a sharp pain in my chest and grasp my chest with my hand. I'm short of breath and my heart is racing like I've just run a marathon.

"A best friend always wants the truth. Talk to me. Are you okay, Emerson?"

"Yeah...I think so." I realize I'm dizzy and lightheaded, so I sit in the chair with my forehead in my hand. Everything seems to be spinning around me.

"You don't look okay. You're sweating and shaking." She looks at another teacher and asks him to get the principal and the nurse.

"Actually, I think you're right, Lauren. I don't feel so great. I'm a little nauseous and I feel like...I feel like everything is closing in on me. I can't breathe." I try to focus on inhaling, but I feel like I can't get any air in my lungs. The room seems to be getting darker and I feel fuzzy all over.

The principal and nurse come into the teacher's lounge and the nurse checks me over.

"I think we need to call an ambulance just to be on the safe side," the nurse says.

"Okay, you do that and I'll call her husband," the principal says as the room goes completely dark.

Owen

My phone rings, and it's a number I don't recognize. I answer anyway because it could be any number of other firefighters I work with calling about paperwork or something else work-related.

"Hello?"

"Mr. Callaghan, this is Principal Jenkins at Chesapeake Elementary School. I'm afraid I have bad news. Your wife has fallen sick and we've had to call an ambulance for her. They are just now leaving with her and taking her to Bay Area Medical Center. The EMTs requested that I ask you to meet her there if possible."

"Of course. Thank you for calling. I'll be right there. Can you send Declan home on the bus? He usually rides home with Emerson."

My heart is in my throat. *What happened?* I shout to the captain that Emerson is on her way to the hospital and I have to go. I don't even wait for an answer. I'm flying out of the station parking lot in no time and make it to the hospital in just a few minutes. I park and run over to the ambulance, where the EMTs are taking Emerson out on a stretcher and into the emergency department. They hand her off to the nurses and I follow them into a room, letting them know I'm her husband.

She's awake and slightly turns her head toward me. She looks so weak. The nurses are taking her vitals, talking about what they think happened and what they need to do.

"What happened? What can I do?" I beg.

"Mr. Callaghan, you'll need to wait in the waiting room while we take care of your wife. We'll update you as soon as possible," one nurse says as another takes my arm and escorts me to the waiting room, where I do not want to be. I crash into the chair and hang my head in my hands, trying to figure out on my own what might have happened. *Did she have a heart attack?* She's been under a lot of stress lately, both at home and at work. Maybe that has something to do with it.

Then I look up and see that it's almost 3:00pm and Keegan will be getting off the bus soon. I'm not ready to talk to Drew, but I have to call him. He's the only one I can think of. I need his help and I know he would want to know about Emerson.

"Hey Callaghan," he answers.

"Drew, I need you," I rasp out. "Emerson got sick at work and they called an ambulance to take her to Bay Area Medical Center."

"Yeah, whatever you need. Is she okay?"

"I think she'll be okay, but they're still assessing her."

"Okay, what can I do?"

"Could you meet the kids at the house and, when Declan gets off the bus, explain what happened and bring them both up here?"

"Yeah man, of course. Call me with any details you get before then, okay?"

"Will do. Thanks, Drew."

I hang up, thankful that at least I don't need to worry about the kids. Time drags on in the waiting room and all sorts of unimaginable circumstances go through my mind. As a firefighter, I'm used to seeing the worst-case scenarios, but not with my family involved in them.

The clock eventually reads 4:30pm and I see Drew coming in the door with Keegan and Declan. I get up and meet them halfway. I hug the kids at the same time. Even though I'm mad at him, I hug Drew, too.

"Thanks for coming up. I appreciate it. They haven't given me any more information since I talked to you. I'm still waiting."

"We'll keep you company while you wait, then," Keegan says. "Mom is tough. She'll be okay." Look at my own kid trying to help me feel better. Keegan has such a big heart.

I head back to my seat. She and Declan sit down on my right, holding hands. Drew takes the seat on the other side of them. We continue waiting and about an hour later, a doctor comes to the waiting room to find us.

"Callaghan Family?" the doctor calls. I immediately stand up, followed by Drew and the kids. My voice is hoarse with emotion. "Yes. We're here. How is she?"

"She's going to be just fine." A collective sigh of relief comes from the whole family. "We've done numerous tests, and the EKG shows us that Emerson's heart is just fine. Her bloodwork came back normal. We were afraid she'd had a heart attack, but we've determined that she had an anxiety attack. We've given her some medicine to help her relax. Please understand that an anxiety attack is no small thing and it can be a precursor to other medical issues. Emerson will need to take some time off work and she'll need help at home so that she doesn't succumb to as much stress as she's been under lately."

I turn and embrace Drew out of sheer gratitude that Emerson is going to be okay. His hug is just as tight as he rubs my back in a comforting motion and then turns to the doctor.

"Thank you, Doctor. Can we see her?" Drew asks the exact question I was thinking.

"Of course. Just two at a time, though, please," he says.

I look at our kids. "Keegan, can you sit out here with Declan while Drew and I go in and see Mom? Then we'll come out and you guys can visit with her."

She gives me a nod and Drew and I walk with the doctor to Emerson's room. She's hooked up to IV fluids and wearing a blue and white hospital gown, but she's awake.

"Sexy gown," I mention with a wink.

"Yeah, thanks a lot." She rolls her eyes.

"What happened? Do you remember anything?" Drew asks. He seems to be the level-headed one in this situation. I'm glad he's here.

She inhales deeply and explains what happened in the teachers' lounge at work, telling us how scary it was and how she thought she was having a heart attack. We're all so thankful that it wasn't a heart attack, but an anxiety attack is serious, too, so we need to make some serious changes.

"We're going to get you home to relax and then we're going to wait on you, hand and foot." I tell her with a gentle hug and a kiss on her forehead. Drew looks at us longingly, as though he wants to do the same thing. I look at Emerson, then at Drew, and nod my head ever so slightly. He hugs Emerson and kisses her forehead, too.

"We're going to make sure you never have that much stress again. I promise. I was so afraid we would lose you. I don't know if I can handle that again. Losing someone I care so much about," Drew says, holding her hand.

Sitting next to her on the other side of the bed, holding her other hand, I tell her, "I promise, too. We'll do whatever we need to, so this never happens again. I'm sure our recent conversations haven't helped any, either, so we'll talk about our relationship as soon as you're comfortable at home and feel like talking."

My eyes find Drew's and he seems grateful that I'm ready to talk about our relationship. I just nod my head because this entire experience with Emerson going to the hospital has opened my eyes. I will not waste any more time worrying about what other people think. Life is too short not to be happy and we're in charge of our own happiness. We're going to make some changes and let our loved ones know we care about them.

Drew and I both hold Emerson one more time and exit to the waiting area. Keegan and Declan visit with their mom for a little while and when they come out, a nurse comes over to us with discharge paperwork, asking for Emerson's husband.

"That's me." I stand. Drew looks like he wants to stand, too, but stays seated. The nurse gives me Emerson's discharge instructions and educates me on anxiety attacks so I can take care of her when we get home. The whole family listens in, though, because we all plan on doting on her as much as necessary until we get our beautiful wife and mom back on her feet. Another nurse strolls out of the emergency department pushing Emerson in a wheelchair and we all load into my truck to head home, except for Drew.

"Is it okay if I meet you guys at the house to help?" Drew asks me cautiously.

"Of course. I wouldn't have it any other way," I tell him, squeezing his shoulder. "We'll see you there."

CHAPTER 16

Drew

On the way back to the Callaghan house, I can't help but think about what life would be like if we'd lost Emerson. It takes me back to the day Corinne was in the hospital and I was just as fearful today as I was then. I am so grateful that Emerson is okay and that we get to take her home to help her heal. Coupled with the fact that it seems like Owen is opening up to the idea of letting me love his family, my heart is exploding right now.

We arrive at the house and file inside one by one, each of us trying to help Emerson along the way.

"Guys! It's okay. I'll be okay. I just need to get inside and lie down to rest. You don't have to do every single thing for me," she admonishes us.

Owen replies first. "We know, but we love you and we don't want anything like this to happen again. I've already called Principal Jenkins to let her know you'll be out for the next two weeks, as per doctor's orders. She said take as much time as you need and she'll take care of writing lesson plans for your sub while you're out."

"That's a huge relief. She's the best. Not many principals would do that. Thank you."

"We're going to make things easier for you around here, Mom," Keegan informs us. This ought to be interesting. "Declan and I will start doing chores like we're supposed to. We need to be more responsible and start helping around the house." Declan doesn't quite seem to be on board, based on the look he gives his sister, but he doesn't argue, so that's a good sign.

"That would be wonderful, Keegan," Emerson gushes.

Once inside, the kids go off to shower and get ready for bed. Owen and I help Emerson to their bedroom. Owen gets her set up with a bubble bath while I turn down the covers and find her comfortable pajamas to sleep in. While Emerson relaxes in the bathtub, Owen and I sit on the bed. There's a silence, but it's comfortable; not awkward like it was after our fight.

"Drew," Owen begins, "I'm sorry. I should have kept an open mind when you were talking to me out in the yard that day. I'm sorry for kicking your ass."

"You didn't kick my ass! I took it like a champ." I give him a side hug. "I'm sorry too, man. I never meant to cause this much trouble."

"Emerson getting sick today is not your fault. Don't think that for one minute. This life is stressful, and she had too much on her plate. I think we can arrange for that to change, though."

"What are you thinking? Can I help?" I hope he's going to include me in this plan to make life better for all of us.

"Well, Grady is moving out, which means we'll have an empty bedroom. Would you be interested in moving in? Making that your bedroom and living here with us? I mean, I'd need to talk to Emerson, and I'd like to run it by the kids, but I think they'd all agree with me."

I am completely shocked. "Do you mean as a platonic roommate, or more?"

"Not platonic, no, but I think we'll have to talk about what things would look like," Owen says humbly.

"Have you had a change of heart? You were dead set against anything I had to say. What changed your mind?" I am so overjoyed that I feel like flying, but I'm trying to contain myself. I know I'm smiling ear to ear like a goofy idiot, but I can't help it.

"I've been thinking about what you and Emerson said. We haven't had a chance to talk, and I'm not sure Emerson will be up for it tomorrow night like we'd planned, but I think we should talk soon. She scared the hell out of me. I've been considering how life could be different if I didn't worry so much about what other people think. We have to live our lives in a way that is best for us, not for other people. What matters is our happiness. I want to know that the people I love are happy and, although I may not show it enough, you're one of the people I love." His eyes meet mine, and I feel a gentle warmth spread over me.

At that moment, Emerson walks out of the bathroom in a plush, white towel, with her hair wrapped in another white towel. She gives us a little look that says she heard what her husband just said. She walks over to him, kisses him on the lips, and says, "I'm so glad you feel that way, Owen."

Owen puts his hands on her hips, probably just to touch her, like I want to do. "I do. I asked Drew if he'd like to move in to Grady's old room. How do you feel about that?" he asks her.

"If you're absolutely sure, I would like that. I love having Drew around the house. I think we still need to sit and talk to iron out some things so that we all end up exactly where we want to be, but I'd love for Drew to move in with us." She sidesteps and wraps her arms around me tightly, kissing my cheek.

I return the simple gesture and hold her just as tightly, telling her gently, "Let's get you into bed."

"So soon?" Owen laughs.

"You know what I mean. She needs to relax. We got your pajamas out for you. Now, put them on and climb into bed."

We get Emerson settled, and it isn't long before she's out like a light. It's been a long, rough day for her, but things are about to change for the better.

Owen

Drew stayed long enough to help get Emerson tucked into bed, but then headed back to the station to get some sleep himself. Crawling into bed with my wife, I just stare at her. I am so lucky to have her in my life. I have three beautiful, intelligent children. Now, my best friend will become part of our family and live with us. I'm still not sure how sensual things will be between me and Drew, but I don't want to keep Emerson and Drew apart. We are capable of loving more than one person at a time, and it's not fair to anyone to withhold love. Life is too short. I've realized that over the last few weeks.

After a restful night, I get up early to get the kids off to school. Keegan heads out the door when the sun hasn't even risen completely yet. While Declan is eating breakfast, Emerson makes her way downstairs and gets comfortable on the couch.

"Babe, can I get you anything?" I ask her.

"I'd love some coffee if you wouldn't mind. Also, when I woke up, I remembered that Declan's teacher called me yesterday before all the commotion. I never got to tell you about it and we never got a chance to talk to Declan about it. When he's done with breakfast, will you ask him to come talk with us in the living room?"

"Sure." I make a cup of coffee for Emerson and bring Declan back with me to sit with her.

"Declan, your teacher called me yesterday," she begins. "She said you've been misbehaving in class. Do you have an explanation for that?"

"I didn't do anything!" Declan shouts and immediately starts crying. His face turns blood red, and he balls up his fists and holds his breath.

"Wait a minute," I tell him. "Calm down. Take a few deep breaths. We can't talk if you're going to shout and cry. Let's talk it out." He looks at me.

"Declan, your teacher said you have been disrupting class, throwing things across the room, and talking when you're not supposed to," Emerson says.

"Declan, is that true?" I ask him.

"No. Everyone else was doing it, not me. Some other kids were not doing it, and I was not doing it." Declan's reply is as clear as mud.

"Then why would your teacher call Mom and tell her you were misbehaving?" I ask him.

"I don't know!" He is refusing to talk now, with an angry look on his face and his fists still balled up.

I try again. "Declan, be honest. Did you throw things and interrupt people when they were learning? Tell the truth."

"Well, I gave a pencil to my friend. And he was at the next group over, so I sort of had to toss it to him."

"That would be considered throwing something across the room. That's dangerous, Dec. You could've hurt someone," Emerson tells him. "Are you talking when you're not supposed to?"

"Well, I was telling Sophie not to talk to me. She won't leave me alone."

"From now on, you raise your hand and tell the teacher if someone is bothering you. Then you won't get in trouble." I stare him down until he nods his head in agreement.

"I don't want to get any more negative calls from your teacher. Is that clear, Declan?" Emerson asks him.

"Yeah."

"Excuse me?" I prod.

"Yes, ma'am. Yes, sir," he says reluctantly.

"Thank you. Now put your shoes on and get down to the bus stop before you miss the bus." Emerson reaches her hands out to hug Declan. Then, he hugs me, puts his shoes on, and he's off to school for the day.

Emerson sips her coffee. I wonder how I'm going to get her to relax all day, much less for two weeks.

***

Drew

"You guys feel like breakfast?" I ask as I come through the front door.

"I thought you had to work today? I could eat. What do you have in mind?" Owen says.

"I took the day off to help you take care of Emerson. Then I stopped by the store on the way here. How about scrambled eggs, hash browns, bacon, and biscuits, just like we do at the station?"

"That sounds delicious. Are you sure you don't mind?" Emerson asks.

"If it'll keep you off your feet and relaxing, then yes. I'll cook three meals a day." I tell her. And I mean it. I would do anything for this woman. I make my way into the kitchen and get started on breakfast. Owen comes in to help and the mouth-watering aromas are floating through the house in no time.

"Everything smells so good, guys," Emerson says as she walks into the kitchen. She puts her arms around Owen and kisses him on the lips. Then she puts her arms around me. We need to take things slowly, so I bend down to kiss her cheek as I wrap my arm around her. She pecks my cheek and heads over to the table. I'm just happy anytime I get to touch her.

"So what are the plans for today?" I ask while I make Emerson a plate.

As I set it down in front of her, she says, "Well, it looks like you guys are going to spoil me rotten. Other than that, I just plan on relaxing; maybe watch a movie or take a nap.

"That sounds like a good day to me," Owen says. "I don't have anything pressing that I absolutely have to do today. I'm learning to prioritize my life. Why don't we all relax with a movie?"

We enjoy breakfast together and talk about what movie we want to watch. Owen offers to clean up while Emerson and I get comfy on the couch and get the movie ready. I walk with my arm around Emerson's waist, as though she might make a run for it, and cover her up with a blanket when she sits.

"Drew, I can do that."

"I know, but I want to do it. Let me take care of you." I sit beside her and kiss her cheek. She reaches for my hand and threads her fingers through mine as though it's the most natural thing. And it is.

Owen joins us on the couch, sitting on the other side of Emerson and taking her other hand. We laze the morning away in our pajamas and watch the movie, getting more tangled in each other as time drifts by. By the end of the movie, Emerson's head is in my lap and her feet are in Owen's lap. We're all as comfortable as we could possibly be. It feels so good to sit here, running my fingers through her hair and kissing her forehead whenever I want to. Owen rubs her thigh and winks at me, letting me know he's just as comfortable with us as I am.

The light snore coming from my lap confirms we aren't alone. Emerson must be just as content as we are. My heart is about to burst.

CHAPTER 17

Emerson

After the movie, and a nap I didn't plan on taking, I wanted to get some fresh air, so I'm hanging out on the back porch reading a book I've had on my 'to be read' list for ages. There's plenty of shade in the backyard, but right now, the gorgeous sun is shining and it feels comforting on my skin.

Drew and Owen step through the back door with three glasses of lemonade and my favorite Pepperidge Farm cookies.

"Thought you might need a snack to finish powering through reading that book," Owen says. They sit down on either side of me at the table and I put my book down.

"How's the story?" Drew asks.

"It's a pretty good book. I'm so glad I have time to read it."

"Hopefully, you'll have much more time in the future," Drew tells me. "I can help out more around the house once I move in completely. Grady's just about finished moving to his new apartment. For the time being, I'll just be here as much as I can. Is there anything we need to take care of for you today?" Drew asks.

"The only thing I can think of is laundry and dinner. I'm sure the laundry is starting to pile up since I was in the hospital yesterday, and of course, we need to make sure we have something to eat later," I tell them. I can't ask for much. They've been wonderful to me.

Owen says, "I'll get the laundry started and then figure out something for dinner."

"Let me take care of dinner," Drew says.

They discuss what to cook and they both go off to take care of laundry and dinner, leaving me relaxing at the table with my book. As they walk by me, they each drop a kiss on my forehead. A girl could get used to this.

Drew

Food is a love language. I don't mind cooking. I'm usually the one cooking at the station if we're all eating together. As Owen heads for the laundry room, I get out the ingredients to marinate a pork roast. As I'm mixing together the olive oil, soy sauce, dijon mustard, and other flavors, Owen leans on the kitchen counter next to me.

"Alright, laundry is going. What can I do to help get dinner ready?" he offers.

"I've got it under control. I'm going to let this pork roast marinate for a few hours and it should be ready to throw on the grill about an hour before dinnertime. We'll throw some potatoes and asparagus on the grill with it, and muah," I put my fingers to my lips and give a chef's kiss in the air.

"Sounds delicious," Owen comments. He seems to have something else on his mind besides dinner, and he continues. "Look, Drew, I appreciate you being here today. I would've been fine taking care of Emerson and doing things around the house by myself today, but I have to say, I like having you here with us." His sincere eyes are focused on mine.

"I like being here with you guys, Owen," I say as I finish up washing the marinade ingredients off my hands and drying them on a towel. I walk over and hug him like we have plenty of times in the past, but this time, it's different. We wrap our arms around each other and the "bro hug" has changed to something a little more intimate. No slapping on the back like we have before. We simply hold each other for a moment, I absorb the heat of his muscles wrapped around me tightly, then I step away with a smile that he returns.

***

We work outside for a while and once the kids have gotten home from school, Emerson soaks in a bubble bath while Owen and I cook dinner. We flow effortlessly around the kitchen preparing our meal and setting the table and in no time, I'm bringing the food in off the grill and we're sitting down as a family to eat together.

I sit beside Owen and across from Emerson. The kids come barreling in the kitchen and immediately start complaining about the asparagus. Declan sits beside me and Keegan sits across the table beside Emerson.

"C'mon, try it," I encourage. "I made it with a special recipe that I bet you've never had before. It doesn't even taste like a vegetable." I laugh as they give in and put one piece of asparagus on their plates with the pork and potatoes. They both try a small bite and although Declan still has a scrunched-up face, Keegan has a surprised face.

"That's actually pretty good, Drew!" She puts more asparagus on her plate. The adults all share a look that says, "Yes! A win!" and we continue on talking about our days and eating. Halfway through dinner, I realize I've put my hand on Owen's thigh and seemed to have left it there unknowingly. I look at my hand, then up to him and he meets my eyes. He gives me a wink that shows he's comfortable and the tension that snuck up on my shoulders releases. Dinnertime is going to be the highlight of a lot of my future days. It sure beats the hell out of eating alone.

Owen

During the last week of February, Emerson hangs out in her comfy clothes and supervises as Drew and I move his belongings into Grady's old room. He has a massive California King Bed, and it makes me want to upgrade my bed, too. He no longer has anything in his storage unit, as everything is now either at our house or in our garage.

The kids were completely comfortable with Drew moving in. They said it only made sense since he's here so much anyway. Grady agreed when he stopped by the next day to check on Emerson. She's been improving every day and we've made sure not to let her do too much or worry about anything.

"I told you Drew ought to just move in to my old room, didn't I?" Grady gloated.

He was right. Drew offered to help pay his share of the bills, which makes things easier on Emerson and I. He'll be home some days when I'm working and vice versa. There are days when we'll both be off work and then there are days that we'll both be working and Emerson and the kids will have the house to themselves. Emerson will probably enjoy some time away from us after all the pampering we've done lately, since we both took days off work to make sure someone was always with her while she's been recovering.

***

THE NEXT FRIDAY AFTERNOON, I head out to the back porch, where Emerson is enjoying the spring-like weather. I sit beside her at the table and ask, "How are you doing?"

"I feel good. It's been a good day. You all have helped me recover and I am so grateful. I'm going back to work on Monday. I wonder...do you think you and Drew might want to talk about our expectations while the kids are still at school?"

"That sounds good. We were waiting until you felt better. Let me go get Drew."

I head into the house and, although I feel a little nervous, I know this is the right thing. It feels right. It may not be what society sanctions or even what my parents will accept, but it's right for us—Me, Emerson, and Drew. We'll figure this out together. I knock on Drew's door and tell him Emerson wants to talk to us.

"'Are we in trouble?" he asks.

"No, you buffoon. She wants to settle everyone's expectations for our relationship. This talk has been a long time coming. I'm ready. How about you?"

"Let's do this," he says with a grin, his eyes sparkling as he gazes at me. A hint of excitement hangs in the air, mixing with the buzz of anticipation. I feel a flutter in my chest as he winks, his playful gesture sending a surge of electricity through me.

I follow him down the stairs and can't help noticing how his confident swagger adds to his charm. On the back porch, I sit beside Emerson at the square table and Drew sits on the other side of her, across from me. We all just sort of look at each other and slowly begin to chuckle at the silliness of it all. Emerson starts for us.

"I'm really glad we're all here and we're going to give *us* a chance. I'm hoping we will be a triad, or a throuple. I care about both of you, and I want the three of us to be equals in this relationship. I don't want it to be open to other people."

With a sigh of relief, Drew agrees. "That's exactly what I was thinking. Although a polyamorous relationship would mean loving multiple people, I only want to be with the two of you in a committed relationship." They both look at me to garner my thoughts.

"I agree. I'm glad we're all on the same page. I've thought about this a lot. I can imagine Emerson loving you, Drew. You're my best friend. If it was anyone else, I wouldn't be comfortable with it. I don't want anyone else to be a part of this, though. I want just the three of us to be committed to one another."

"That sounds perfect," Emerson murmurs. "We've been getting along well so far. We've spent so much time together that when Drew moved in, it was just a natural progression and we all blend well together. The kids love that he's here." She thinks for a moment before she says, "Should I broach the subject of...nevermind."

"Talk to us. You have to be open and honest with us, Emerson. That's the only way this can work. That's the only way Drew and I will know what's going on in your mind."

"Please tell us what you're thinking. Are you wondering about how things will go sexually?" Drew says.

"Well, yes. I like the extra affection I've been getting from both of you. Will we all be intimate with each other? Will I be with both of you at different times?" She hesitates for a moment, thinking of the right words. "Will you two be affectionate toward each other?" Emerson blushes a little.

"What do you want? Tell us what would be the perfect relationship for you and then Drew and I will tell you our opinions."

"I would like to be with both of you, either at the same time or separately, whichever you're both comfortable with. I'm comfortable with the two of you being together alone or with me, whatever you both want," she tells us. I squeeze her hand because I know it's taking a lot of courage for her to say these things to her husband and the other man she cares for. I'm not sure I'm quite ready to speak, so I motion for Drew to go ahead with his thoughts.

"I'm comfortable being with either or both of you, both together and separately," he says, "but only if we're all content with what we decide."

My turn.

"Of course, I love to be with Emerson, and I'm comfortable with the two of you being together alone, if that's what you both want. With the way we work, there will be times when it's impossible for all three of us to be here at the same time. If the two of you are here alone, I'm okay with you being intimate without me. I think I need some time to figure out exactly what I want with you, Drew. That's going to have to be something we explore because it's a new concept to me. I'm trying to keep an open mind. I'd like to see how things go with all three of us together and go from there, if that's okay with you guys."

Our companionable relationship now has set sexual expectations and boundaries. I look at Emerson and Drew and blurt out, "How did I get this lucky?" I lean over to kiss my wife, and knowing Drew is watching us, turns me on. I slide my tongue against hers and wonder if I'll ever do this with Drew. When we finish kissing, Drew and I look at each other and Emerson looks back and forth at both of us. My eyes meet Drew's and I tilt my head toward Emerson. Drew leans in to kiss her for the first time, knowing I'm watching as well. It's a slow, gentle, lingering kiss, like they've been waiting their whole lives for it. I see him tasting her tongue and, again, I wonder what it might be like to kiss him. Damn, that turns me on even more. They end their kiss with a longing look into each other's eyes.

"I always thought seeing my wife kiss another man would make me angry, but that's not the case."

"I'm curious. How does it make you feel?" Emerson asks.

I stand, pulling her and Drew by the hands so we're all standing together.

"I feel like I'm part of something incredibly special. I'm going to do whatever I can to make it last."

And with that sentiment, the kids come bouncing out the door to see what we're up to. Our alone time has now turned into family time. That happens abruptly when there are kids involved. I am anxious to find out what happens when we get more alone time, though. Judging by the coy looks on their faces, I think Drew and Emerson are, too.

Chapter 18

WE'VE ALL FALLEN INTO a comfortable routine by the end of March. I've been back in my classroom for a few weeks now, and the guys have both gotten back into their regular schedules at work, plus the overtime days.

When I get home from work on Friday, the kids are already there. Keegan is in her room and Declan is in the game room playing Minecraft. Drew is cooking dinner, so I walk up behind him at the stove and place my arms around his waist from behind. "Hi there. How was your day?"

"It was good," he says. "I'm glad you're home." He puts a top on the pot and turns around to place his arms around me.

His gorgeous blue eyes look down at me, and his lips meet mine for a gentle kiss.

"Dinner will be ready in just a few minutes. I made Chicken Parmesan. Are you hungry?"

"Definitely. Thank you for cooking. I want to go check in with the kids first, though." He nods and I head to Keegan's bedroom where she is always either on the phone or reading a book. Right now, it's the latter. I give a quick knock on the partially open door and she tells me I can come in.

"Hey, Sweetie. Drew is cooking dinner, so I have some time to chat. Just wanted to check on you. How are things going?" I sit down on the bed beside her where she's sprawled out reading her book.

"I guess things are fine. Guys are stupid, you know?"

"Oh yes, I know. But why are they stupid this time? Did something happen?"

"Remember the guy I told you about? I thought he liked me, but he wouldn't talk to me at school. He would only text with me or talk on the phone after school. I talked to Drew about it and he said I should talk about it with Lee and find out why."

"He's right. Did you talk to Lee?"

"Yeah. He didn't want to explain anything, but I eventually figured out he was embarrassed to be seen with me in public. He said he really likes me, but I'm not really one of the cooler kids in school, so he just wanted to be my boyfriend after school when it was just us."

Drew pops his head in the door to let us know dinner is ready.

"You talked to the guy?" he asks Keegan.

"Yes. He was embarrassed to be seen with me in public. I told him if he really cared about me, he would be proud to be seen with me in public. I also told him I didn't want to talk to him anymore."

Drew smiles, "That's good, Keegan. I'm glad you talked to him and stood up for yourself. Any guy would be lucky to have you as a girlfriend." He comes in and hugs her. "Just don't go getting married on us anytime soon, okay? Let's go eat."

Drew, Keegan, Declan and I sit at the kitchen table to eat and share about our days.

"Declan, how was school today? What did you guys do?" I ask.

"It was boring, just like every other day. We're learning about the water cycle, so we did an experiment in Science class where we put water in a bottle and put it on the counter in the sun. We read an article and did some other stuff and then looked at our bottles again."

"Sounds interesting," I say. "What happened?"

"Well, water drops evaporated into the air and stuck to the top of the bottle. It was supposed to show us how the water cycle works."

"That's cool. Do you know what it's called when the water droplets stick to the top of the bottle?"

"Con...Concen...no. I can't remember."

"Condensation," Drew mentions. "We have to know all about the water cycle as firefighters."

"You do?" Now Declan seems a little more intrigued.

"Yes. Sometimes when we put out a fire, we use water, so we have to know all the properties of water and how it behaves, so we know the most efficient way to put the fire out."

Keegan chimes in on the conversation. "Wait a minute. You said sometimes you use water. Do you use other things?"

"Sure do. Sometimes we have to use a special foam to put out certain types of fires. We'll use whichever is more effective. Sometimes water can make a fire worse, like when there's a grease fire in the kitchen." The kids now think he's a genius.

We finish dinner and the kids clean up while Drew and I sit on the back porch. It's warmer now that Spring has begun and we only have a couple months left of school. Drew sits on the bench and motions for me to sit beside him.

When I do, he wraps his arm around my shoulders, and I snuggle into him. Gazing at the stars in the clear night sky, I think about how lonely it was sometimes to be the only adult at home when it was just me and Owen. I'm starting to realize that despite our deep love for each other, there was a certain element lacking in our relationship. Drew strengthens and completes our relationship.

Hand in hand, looking at his handsome face, I say, "Drew, I'm so glad you're here with us."

Drew smiles with that dimple of his and simply says, "Me, too." He leans in, putting his hand on my neck, rubbing my cheek with his thumb. He pulls me closer to him and brushes his kissable lips against mine. When his tongue touches my bottom lip, shivers run up my spine. He's an amazing kisser. Owen is too, but they kiss differently.

We're not worried about the kids seeing us kiss because after our talk, we had a family discussion about the changes that have happened. The kids love Drew and they're happy he's living with us. I'm so glad they were open to Owen and I changing our relationship to include Drew. He's such a good man, and now I am lucky enough to have two good men.

"I was thinking," Drew begins. "Since Owen is working, do I get to sleep with you tonight?"

"I think that can be arranged," I reply with a grin.

We've gotten into a routine of sorts. If Owen is home at night, I sleep in our bed with him. If he's working, I still sleep in our bed by myself, but Drew will come tuck me in at night. A couple times, he laid down with me until I fell asleep, then went to his bedroom. That was much better than falling asleep by myself, but I'd love to share the bed with him all night long. We haven't all slept in the same bed together. I wonder if we will get to that point. Owen has really come around and I would savor sleeping between my men.

"I don't think we should be too intimate without Owen here with us for our first time, though." I have dreamt of that night many times.

"I completely agree." He kisses my nose. "I'd love to hold you in my arms as we fall asleep, though. Maybe get a few extra kisses..." he trails off as he kisses first one cheek, then the other. He wraps his arms around me, pulls me tight to his chest, and kisses me slowly; a lingering, passionate kiss that shows rather than tells how he feels about me.

Before our kiss gets a little too hot, he pulls back. "Maybe we should wait and finish this when we go to bed."

"I think that's a good idea. Let's get the kids to bed."

Drew tucks the kids in while I make sure all the doors are locked and the lights are off. I grab some pajamas from my dresser and head to the bathroom to take a shower before turning in. I turn on the water and, when it's at the right temperature, I start to take off my shirt, but the door gradually creaks open. Drew pokes his head in and slowly saunters into the bathroom.

"May I help you with that?" he says with a smirk. He takes off my shirt and is clearly admiring my top half as he moves his hands to my waist. He unbuttons my jeans and pulls the zipper down. Then he crouches down in front of me and slowly pulls them down my legs until they hit the floor. I brace myself on his shoulders and step out of them, one foot at a time. I can feel his heated gaze from my feet all the way up my body until he meets my eyes.

He stands again and reaches around me to unclasp my bra as he raises an eyebrow to see if I'm comfortable. I kiss him to let him know I am very comfortable. He unclasps my bra and slides it down my arms, all the while taking in my breasts.

"God, you're gorgeous, Emerson." When my bra hits the floor, his hands come up to feel my breasts, and he leans down to suck on my nipple. His warm mouth feels so good on my skin as he moves to the other nipple and gives it the same attention.

He looks into my eyes and hooks his index fingers in the top of my panties. He slowly starts moving them down my legs until he's kneeling in front of me, and I step out of them. He shoves them in his pocket with a sly grin.

He continues to kneel in front of me, just looking up at my body, as if it's the most beautiful thing he's ever seen. I start to get a little nervous because now I'm completely bare to him and I've got curves from three children, a mar-riage, and lots of time passing. I move my hands to cover myself and he catches them and intertwines his fingers with mine, placing my hands beside me against the wall so he can still see everything.

"Please don't hide yourself from me, Emerson. Your body is exquisite. Everything about you—inside and out—is absolutely perfect. I wouldn't change a single thing about you. It is killing me not to take you right here, but that's not how I want to make love to you for the first time."

Reluctantly, he starts to stand up, but he can't resist running his tongue from my belly button up through my breasts to my neck as he stands.

He looks from my lips to my eyes as he says, "I have to leave now, or I won't be able to restrain myself any longer, and I want Owen to be here for our first time. I'll shower downstairs and meet you in bed." He gives me a playful kiss on the nose and reluctantly leaves the bathroom. I have to take several deep breaths to keep from passing out.

How did I get so lucky?

Chapter 19

I MUST BE DREAMING. Standing in the shower—downstairs by myself, of course—I can't help but think I must be dreaming. I never thought I'd find anyone else. I thought I'd had one love in my life and I lost both her and Michael. How could I possibly get the chance to love again in one lifetime? Not just one person this time, but two loves of my life and three beautiful children that I consider my own. So, this must be a dream; one where this angelic woman has blessed me with her love. I'm hoping her husband will do the same, but I won't push him. I hope one day for Emerson to be my wife, too, and Owen to be my husband. Legally, we can't make it official, but we can still have a ceremony and it will be real to the three of us. I want them both for the rest of my life.

After my cold shower to put things back in perspective, I dry off, pull on a pair of shorts, and walk upstairs to get in bed. Emerson will sleep with me tonight, for the first time. That's all I want to do—sleep—because our first time making love needs to be with Owen. I can't wait to lie beside her and hold her in my arms.

Emerson is just coming out of the bathroom as I ascend the stairs. She grasps my outstretched hand, entangling her fingers with mine as we make our way into my bedroom. I pull the covers down so she can crawl under them and I feel as excited as a little kid on their birthday morning, waiting to see what great surprises are in store.

When Emerson's comfortable, I go around the bed and crawl under the covers, too, trying not to dive right in and show how anxious I am. I make my way to the middle of my king-sized bed to wrap my arms around her tight, facing her. Looking into the depths of her blue eyes, I realize I am completely lost to this woman. *I never want to let her go.*

Running my fingers through her hair, I tell her, "Emerson, I love you. I don't know how I got so lucky, but I'm going to do everything I can to make sure our relationship—you, Owen, and me—lasts forever."

She smiles at me. "I love you, too, Drew. I thought I was happy before you came into our lives, but I realize now that there was something missing. With you, it's like all the pieces of the puzzle are finally together and I never even knew there were any missing."

I gently kiss her lips, a slow, warm, lingering kiss that hopefully communicates a little of the emotion I'm feeling that I can't quite put into words.

"I am so glad you feel that way. How is Owen feeling about us?" I ask.

"He's been quiet. It seems he's been doing a lot of thinking lately. I said the same thing to him, about a missing puzzle piece, and he nodded in agreement. He admitted it's strange that we thought we had everything, but when he realized you could be more than a best friend, it opened his eyes to a new, more satisfying reality. He cares a lot for you."

"He means the world to me. When I first moved here to Virginia, he was the first guy at the station to help me out, taking me under his wing and making sure I had everything I needed. He's been there for me since my first shift at the station and we've grown closer every day since. We have so much in common, and now we have you in common," I say with a smirk.

"Yes, you do." Her hand caresses my cheek. "You have each other, too."

"He's my best friend. Is it selfish to want more with him?"

"No, not at all. Give him some time. I think he's coming around to the idea." Her lips find mine in the moonlight. "I'm hoping you two will be more than best friends, too."

We talk and hold each other until the late night hours, when we finally force ourselves to go to sleep. Holding Emerson in my arms, I get the best sleep I've had in over ten years. The only thing that would make this night better would be to have Owen in bed with us.

Owen

When I walked in the door this morning, Drew was on his way out.

With a fist bump, he says, "Hey, man, I'm headed to the volunteer station for a while. I have some things to take care of there; some training and the engine needs to be cleaned after the late night call we had last night."

"Sounds good. Let me know if you need any help. When do you think you'll be back?" I ask him.

"I should be back in a couple of hours. I have no other plans today."

"Good, because I was hoping we could hang out with Emerson today. My parents are taking the kids for the weekend, so it's just the three of us."

When he smiles, a flicker of heat passes through his gaze at me, and he says, "Awesome! In that case, someone else can wash the engine. I can't wait. I'll get back as soon as I can." His thick arms wrap around my neck and shoulders as he pulls me against his body. I slide my arms around him and hug his trim waist, rubbing his muscular back. He backs away too soon, leaving me wanting, and the sparkle in his eye says we're not finished yet as he backs up toward the door.

I watch him as he leaves for the station, wondering what these feelings are and if I'll ever get used to them. Drew brings something out in me—feelings I never knew were there—and for once, I feel like I'm complete.

After tossing my wallet and keys on the counter like I always do, I walk upstairs to say good morning to Emerson, but she's not in our bed. She wasn't downstairs when I came in, so there's only one other likely place she'd be. I make my way to Drew's bedroom and find her snuggled up under the covers. I climb in on his side of the bed, his scent enveloping me intoxicatingly. I align myself with Emerson's curves and wrap my arms around her. The mesmerizing blend of Drew's sandalwood cologne and Emerson's patchouli lotion overwhelms my senses. The only other thing I want right now is for Drew to hold me the way I'm holding Emerson.

"Mmmm...." she moans seductively. "How fortunate am I to have one handsome man leave, only to have another come home and put his arms around me?"

My lips brush along her neck, her cheek, all the way to her mouth. "Good morning, Beautiful. Did you have a good night?"

"Yes, I did, but we didn't do anything without you. We just talked and cuddled. Drew wants you to be a part of our first time," she says.

"I'm looking forward to it. That's why I've talked to my parents about taking them up on their offer for the kids to spend the weekend with them. They were going to months ago, but in all the chaos, it never happened. They're happy to get some quality time with their grandkids. I think we deserve a weekend to ourselves."

"What about Drew?"

"Drew is taking care of some things at the volunteer station and then he should be home by late morning. I'll get the kids ready and drop them off at my parents' house. By the time we both get back, we'll be able to spend most of today, tonight, and tomorrow together." She sighs at the thought of finally getting some alone time with both of us.

Emerson

Saturday is the only day of the week that I really get to clean. I try to get as much done as I can on Saturday or else the guys have to do it during the week when they're home from work. I try not to leave them too much to do. I've already washed two loads of laundry today, and I have another one going. Now, I'm dusting, and cleaning the floors is next. I don't mind vacuuming, but sweeping and mopping are my least favorite chores. As soon as I finish, I think I'll pack a lunch for the three of us. It's such a nice, warm day that I can't imagine staying inside.

Our lunch is all packed by the time the guys—my guys—get back home. Owen walks in the door first.

"Wow, the house looks great, Babe. You didn't have to do all this. Drew and I can work on chores during the week. What's this?" he asks, pointing to the picnic basket.

"It's a dinosaur," I say with a serious face.

"Smartass. I know what it is. Why is it here?" He rolls his eyes at me.

"It's so nice out today. I thought we'd have a picnic outside. What do you think?"

"That sounds good. Where do you want to go?"

"Oh, I was just thinking we could hang out in the backyard."

Drew walks in and says, "What are we doing in the backyard?"

"I'd like for all three of us to enjoy the sunshine and have lunch," I tell him.

"That sounds good, but let's get away from the house for a while. How about we eat down by beach? I'm sure the water's still slightly too cold to go swimming since it's just barely May, but we could still enjoy the view," Drew suggests.

"I'd love that."

We take our lunch and a big blanket to Owen's truck, climb in, and buckle up in the front seat with me in the middle of my two guys. Owen drives and puts his right arm around my shoulders. Drew casually rests his left hand on my leg. I am cherishing being with them and having them all to myself.

We haven't really been out together in public yet, so I'm not sure how this will go. People in general aren't too accepting of anything that is different from their norm, so there's a chance we could experience some people making rude comments or even just some degrading looks. That's fine by me. They don't have to understand my relationship, but they do have to respect it. I will not let anyone ruin our day because they can't understand how we feel. Just because our relationship is different than theirs, that doesn't mean it's wrong.

CHAPTER 20

PARKING AT THE BEACH, we get a great spot because there aren't too many people here. One car is in the same parking lot, but I don't see anyone on or near the water. A couple of trucks are parked over at the boat ramp, empty boat trailers hitched to the trucks. They could be watermen that are still out, bringing in their catch for the day.

I take Emerson's hand to help her down out of the truck, and we make our way over to the picnic tables in the grassy park area. There's a slight breeze blowing through the trees that makes Emerson's sundress flutter around her luscious thighs. I'd give anything to have them wrapped around my waist right now.

I spread out a tablecloth on one of the picnic tables and we all work to unpack our lunch. I sit beside Emerson, and Owen sits across from us.

"Thanks for putting this lunch together for us, Em. It's nice to get out of the house." I place my hand on the small of Emerson's back and lean in to give her a kiss on the cheek.

Owen nods in agreement, looking at us the same way Emerson looks at chocolate cake. *What is he thinking?*

As she pours us each a cup of iced tea, Emerson asks, "How are things going at the station?"

"About the same," I tell her, piling food on my plate.

"Did you know they interviewed that chick, Cate, that Nick was dating?" Owen adds.

"Really?" Emerson and I say simultaneously.

"Yeah, apparently, she put in an application for a fire-fighter/EMT spot. Chief says the girl has no experience, but is ate up with the fire station, the equipment, all of it. At her interview, she wanted to show him she can do the Stair Climb and Hose Drag portions of the Physical Ability Test. He told her she'd get to that if she passed the second round of interviews. Chief said she was asking tons of questions about the calls we run, and he had to tell her it wasn't something they could discuss in an interview."

"Wow," I mutter, "that girl was strange when we met her a few months ago, but this takes it up a notch. I wonder if she applied so she can be closer to Nick more often. Is Nick still dating her?"

"I have no idea," Owen replies. "If so, I hope he sees the light soon. I don't know about that one."

"You know who else I thought was a little strange?" I ask. They look at me with raised eyebrows while they're chewing, so I continue, "Lamont. Lauren's husband. Emerson, what's going on with them? Are they okay?"

"I don't know," she says, sadly. "Lauren has talked to me about it, but I don't know all the details. I know she's not happy right now, and hasn't been for a while. She's doing her best to shelter the kids from it. I feel bad for her."

"I do, too. At the cookout we had at your place—-our place, now," I say with a smirk, "Lamont didn't want to talk to anyone. He said he didn't want to come that day and when I offered to make sure Lauren and the kids got home safely so he could leave to do whatever he needed to do, he acted like he couldn't trust her to leave her alone. Or maybe he couldn't trust me."

"He's never really liked firefighters, so you may be right. Maybe he didn't want to leave her with a bunch of firefighters, not that I can blame him," she says, winking at us. "He won't let her do anything. He has to know where she is, what she's doing, and especially who she's with if she's not at home.

"And you know what else gets me?" Emerson pauses like she's connecting the dots. "She told me he's at work all day and won't join her for lunch, even though he gets an hour for his lunch break every day. Then, he comes home for dinner and leaves again right away. He tells her he has something to do at the office or a meeting with someone. It's just strange."

"It sounds like it," Owen agrees. "I hope they figure it out and things get better. Let Lauren know we're here if she needs anything."

"I will. So what do you think about our picnic? Getting full yet?" Her bright eyes await our approval.

"These deviled eggs are delicious, Babe," Owen says. "You know they're one of my favorites."

I take one of my deviled eggs and hold it up to Emerson's mouth. Her eyes meet mine as she takes a bite, licks her lips, and then I eat the rest of the egg.

"Mmm...delicious," I agree. Emerson reaches forward to wipe a little something off my lip and I lick it off her finger, just like she did that day in the fire station.

"Speaking of delicious," Owen says, "Emerson, you look gorgeous in that dress. I love when the weather warms up and I get to see more of your body."

"If you don't stop talking like that," I say with a low growl, "our picnic won't be rated G for long. My jeans are already getting tighter just thinking about Emerson's legs in that dress." I slide my hand along her waist, up her back, and grasp her neck, pulling her to me for a kiss.

"I had no idea you guys were such leg men," she says with a laugh. "I'll have to keep that in mind."

"Honey, we like everything on your body," Owen declares.

We talk, flirt, and feed each other as the afternoon goes on. I watch longingly as Emerson gently places grapes between Owen's lips. Then she slips cucumber slices in my mouth. I've never been so at ease with anyone before. It's like the three of us have known each other our whole lives.

Owen

Drew watched as Emerson fed me grapes, and their dual attention turned me on. Then she fed Drew cucumber slices, and I understood why he had that look on his face. Watching her feed him, put food in his mouth, between his lips, was one of the most erotic things I've ever watched and she didn't even intend for it to be.

Seeing Emerson and Drew together, holding hands and kissing, makes me feel like we are finally complete.

"You guys want to go for a walk?" I ask. Even though lunch is done, I don't want this afternoon to end.

"That sounds wonderful," Emerson says.

Drew is the first to grab her hand since he's sitting beside her, and they stand. As I stand up, I grab the blanket Emerson brought and throw it over my shoulder, just in case we need it.

The three of us walk toward the boardwalk and it's wide enough for all of us, so I grab Emerson's other hand and we venture over to the water. Looking down through the wooden slats, we can see the sand and marsh beneath us, as well as initials others have carved into the handrails. It makes the kid in me want to carve

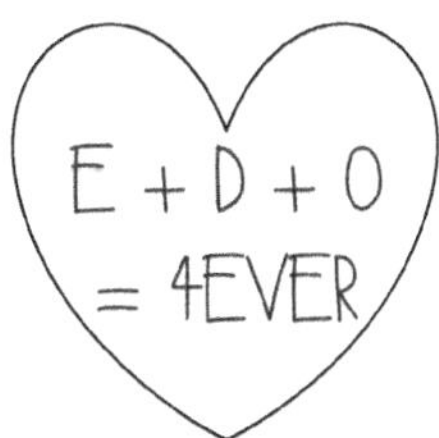

into the wood as we stroll along the boardwalk.

The weather is warm, and the breeze feels wonderful. I can see the river past the dunes and marsh, but I'm more interested in looking at Emerson and Drew. I never thought I'd want another person in our relationship.

Drew's been my best friend ever since he came to Virginia, but I hadn't thought of him as more than a friend until he mentioned something to Emerson. I've always thought he was a handsome, respectable man. When I found out he was interested in me as more than a friend and wanted to share Emerson, I was shocked, but it makes sense. Eventually, I got over my ego and opened my mind to the possibility of a triad relationship, and now it just feels right that he's a part of us.

After walking along the sand for a few minutes, we come to an opening between the dunes where we can see the horizon miles away. Our trio stands there, simply admiring the beauty of the land meeting the river and the river meeting the sky.

Drew and I look into each other's eyes, and then at Emerson. She looks back and forth between us. I drop the blanket to the ground and gently tug on her hand to pull her close enough that her body is just an inch away from mine. While she's still holding both of our hands, I tilt her chin up with my other hand and dip my head down to kiss her lips. A low growl comes from behind Emerson, and Drew eases closer to us to forge the perfect triangle. I end our kiss and gaze at Emerson and Drew.

Drew leans forward, taking Emerson's lips and tasting her as he intertwines his fingers in mine. There's no one else around to hear the groan that escapes my chest while I watch them kiss. When he's had his fill of Emerson, he turns his gorgeous blue eyes to me with a smirk.

"Owen," Drew begins in a ragged voice, "I want to kiss you." My blood heats with just those few words. There's a question in his eyes as he looks from my eyes to my mouth and when I don't argue or look away, he slowly takes my face in both hands and places an easy, lingering kiss on my lips. I return the kiss while I close my eyes and enjoy it because, hell, he feels incredible. I open my eyes to his, staring back at me with hope. He lowers his hands and stands in front of me, waiting. It seems as though he's leaving the ball in my court, so to speak.

My hands move on their own to Drew's waist, up his chest, and to his neck. I pull him to me and kiss him, gently at first. I know my wife is watching us and her arousing moan urges me on. It feels so good kissing him that I want more, so I tilt my head and open my mouth, just barely licking his bottom lip. His mouth opens for me and we taste each other for the first time. Drew's hands move to my back, caressing me. Our kiss turns more passionate and our bodies are pressed against each other in a way that makes it impossible to ignore how hard Drew is for me. My khakis are just as tight as our kiss slowly comes to an end, as though neither of us wants it to.

We simply hold on to each other, staring into each other's eyes as Emerson sighs and says, "That was the hottest thing I've ever seen." She giggles and puts her arms around both of us. Drew and I nod in agreement and we wrap our arms around her to pull her in for a group hug that will forever be cemented in my memories.

"I don't want today to end," Emerson says. "How about we spread out the blanket and enjoy the view?"

"Sounds good to me," Drew says. "I'd love to sit and look at you. The sun will be setting soon, too."

She smacks his chest, saying, "You know I meant the sun."

I spread out the blanket and Emerson sits in the middle with her men on either side of her, staring out into the river. Looking out at the horizon makes me feel like there are endless possibilities in life now. Thinking back, I was so closed-minded when Drew accidentally let his feelings escape. Now, looking at us, I am so glad he did.

Drew

I was a complete dumbass when I accidentally told Emerson how I felt about her, but do I regret it? Hell, no. We wouldn't be here, together, like this, if it weren't for me being a dumbass.

Looking at these two amazing people in front of me, I still can't believe they're mine. They're both gorgeous in the dimming sunlight and my heart is full of emotions as I sit here and appreciate them.

"Emerson," I say, looking at her. "Owen," I say, looking at him. "I love you both with all of my heart."

Emerson smiles and kisses me as Owen holds my hand. "I love you both, too," she says. "I feel like I'm in a dream that I never want to end."

"We'll do our best to never let it end, Baby," Owen promises. "I love you both."

We sit in comfortable silence, listening to the waves lapping at the beach and the seagulls flying overhead. We watch as the sun starts to descend beyond the horizon, the many colors in the sky changing from blue and green to orange and red as day becomes night.

Chapter 21

SPENDING THE DAY WITH Owen and Drew has been absolutely wonderful. Watching the sunset with them was so romantic, but that kiss. When I witnessed them kiss for the first time, my heart melted. Now, they've insisted we have dinner at a local riverside restaurant, which is even better.

Nervously, I ask, "What will people think when they see the three of us together?" I don't normally worry about what others think, but our relationship has become concrete and I don't want to hide anything. I want to be sure that the guys feel the same way.

"Well, I can tell you what the men will think. They'll think Drew and I are fucking lucky to have a gorgeous woman dine with us and wonder how we did it," Owen says as he puts his arm around my waist. Drew locks his fingers in mine and we walk up to the hostess stand. They are clearly not concerned about what other restaurant patrons might think of us.

The hostess leads us to a round table on the outside deck, and Owen pulls a chair out for me. Then, they both take a seat on either side of me. Sitting outside the restaurant, we can see the lightning bugs flickering and the stars twinkling in the sky. The sounds of the river are relaxing. We can hear boats off in the distance and the chattering of people night fishing off the pier. While we enjoy the view, the server brings our drinks and we order our appetizers and meals.

"Earlier, you guys told me the chief interviewed Cate and some others, but have they actually hired any new firefighters at the station?" I ask while we wait for our food. "I can't wait to have you guys home with me and the kids more often."

"They hired ten new people and they're supposed to start the fire academy soon. Not everyone will make it through, but we're hoping to get at least eight new firefighters on the floor in a few months." Owen knows how much I miss them when they're at work.

"Yeah, that should help with the overtime," Drew adds. "Things would be easier on us if this firebug would stop."

"Have you heard anything more about the investigation?" I can't imagine why anyone would want to set things on fire for absolutely no reason.

Drew shakes his head. "The local and state police are investigating, and they're working with the arson investigator's office. So far, there have been eight incidents of brush fires that we've been called out to. What's worse is that the fires are getting closer to residential homes, which could be dangerous. I don't get why someone has to go around starting fires for fun, draining emergency personnel and resources, but to start them close to homes is a whole other ball game."

The server brings our food and we start to dig in.

"Have they gotten any leads?" I ask.

"If they have, they haven't made it public," Owen says between bites. "They've found evidence of accelerants and similar burn patterns with each fire. So far, it looks like they've all been started the same way. If it's not the same person setting all the fires, it's multiple people who are discussing what they're doing. The last fire was so close to the West's barn that it burned one wall down. Whoever this is, they're getting more brazen with each fire."

"That's terrible! I hope they figure it out soon. I'm sure it's wearing on the emergency responders."

Drew nods his head. "It's been hard, but we're getting through it." He takes my hand in his and gently kisses my knuckles. "Let's not worry about that right now. What should we do after dinner?"

"It's getting kind of late," I say. "Maybe we could go home and watch a movie?"

As Drew starts to answer me, we hear snickering from the next table over that draws our attention.

"I wonder what kind of movie they'll watch?" the guy says.

"Probably one of those pornos with LGBTABCD people in it," the snotty girl across from him says. "At least they'll be leaving soon."

"I can't believe they would even come out in public and not hide the fact that they're all sleeping around. It's sickening," he replies.

Finally, Drew can't take any more of their ignorant shit, so he stands up and walks over to them. I look at Owen in fear, afraid of what Drew might do, and he takes my hand in his to comfort me.

"What's sickening," Drew says to them pointedly as he puts his fists on the table and leans over to them so other customers won't hear, "is the fact that you all are so closed-minded that you can't let other people live and love without ridiculing them for being brave enough to be themselves and find happiness. You don't have to understand our relationship, but you do need to either respect us or shut the hell up. We're not hurting you. You have no right to judge and berate us for something you know nothing about."

Leaving them with their mouths hanging open and eyes as big as half dollars, Drew sits back down at our table like nothing happened.

Right at that moment, the server appears and asks, "Would you all like dessert this evening?"

Owen answers for all of us, saying, "No, thank you. I think we'll have dessert at home. I'll take the check when it's ready."

Owen pays and my guys walk me out to the truck, both of them proudly holding my hands.

"Drew, why don't you drive home tonight?" Owen suggests, tossing him the keys. Owen opens the door for me and helps me into the middle seat, then hops in beside me. When we're all buckled in, Drew backs out of the parking lot and drives us home with his right hand on my thigh.

Owen's left hand is resting on my other thigh, and I notice that it's slowly starting to creep up. I take a glance at him and he has a heated look on his face that clearly tells me what's on his mind. He shifts his body toward me, moving his left hand up to my face.

"Emerson, I've wanted you all day." His right hand moves to my knee. "I plan on having you for dessert when we get home. I want to make sure you're ready for us." He pulls my head toward his as he kisses me like he's starving and I'm the first meal he's had in days. His right hand slowly moves up the inside of my thigh until he reaches my panties. He draws tiny circles on my panties, teasing me, until he finally ends our kiss. I know he can feel how damp they are. He looks over at Drew, who is trying hard to focus on the road.

"Good thing we're almost home. I can see Drew wants a taste of you, too."

"Damn right, I do." Drew slides his right hand under my dress, puts his hand right where Owen's is, and feels my pussy through my panties. At the same time, they each dip their finger under my panties and slide through my folds.

"Owen, I think she's ready for us."

"She's soaked. I can't wait to get her home. How about we sleep in your bed tonight since it's bigger? It'll give us more room."

I let out a little moan and mumble, "I thought we were going to watch a movie tonight?"

"Oh, no, Emerson. It's time for Owen and me to have our dessert. We've waited long enough for this." All I can do is sigh as they both spread my wetness through my folds. Drew slides his finger inside of me, making me tip my head back against the seat and moan out loud. Owen tugs on my clit like he wishes it was his mouth sucking on it, then he leans over to lick and suck my neck, right below my ear, and it makes me come undone. With an aroused moan, I hold on tight to their thighs as my orgasm takes over. I can feel my insides clenching on Drew's finger and everything starts to dim as I close my eyes and enjoy the ride. I see tiny sparkles as my orgasm reaches its height and I want to stay there forever.

I start to come down, my breathing slows, and I open my eyes to look at Owen and Drew. I don't know how we got here, but we're in the driveway at home and Owen is picking me up to carry me inside. I wrap my arms around his neck as he carries me to Drew's bed. Drew pulls back the covers and Owen gently lays me down. He kisses me, then backs away and rubs Drew's back as Drew bends to kiss me.

"Emerson, rest for a bit, Baby. I'll keep Owen occupied until your energy comes back." With a smirk, Drew takes Owen's hands and pulls him toward him for a tentative kiss, almost as if he's asking permission. Owen slides his arms around Drew and kisses him back, freely giving that permission. After all my energy was drained with that orgasm in the truck, all I can do is lay here and watch them, and there's nothing I'd rather watch more.

Owen

Drew is considerate about kissing me until I kiss him back. He doesn't want to push me into doing anything I'm not ready for, and that's one of the reasons I love him.

I cup Drew's face in my hands and look longingly into his handsome blue eyes. I can't get enough of him, yet I want to try. I want to explore him with all of my senses. Bringing his stubbled jaw to mine, I kiss him tenderly on his full lips, beside his lips, his cheek, anywhere I can, just to taste him.

Tilting my head, I kiss his lips more roughly and he opens his mouth to me, taking the back of my head in his hands, like he wants to keep me there. Sliding my tongue into his hot mouth, I memorize this feeling of passion overtaking me in this intimate, seductive moment. The warmth washes over me and I never want to let this man go.

My wife lays sedated on the bed, watching me kiss Drew, and judging by her moans and Drew's, this is one night we won't soon forget. Knowing Emerson is here while I'm exploring Drew turns me on even more. It's like this relationship couldn't exist with just me and Drew. We need Emerson in this dynamic to make it perfect. That's not to say I'll never make love to Drew without Emerson. She's already told us she is comfortable with that, and as turned on as I am right now, I'm sure it'll happen eventually.

The more Drew and I kiss, the hotter it gets. Our tongues tangle and hands roam each other's body. He tugs on my shirt like it's in the way, so I take it off and then pull his off, too. I grab his waist and pull his body flush to mine so he can feel exactly how much I want him. As I slide my hands up his back, feeling his muscles tighten, he cups my ass and pushes his hips against me so hard that I groan with desire. I've been hard since we got in the truck and Drew's hand brushed mine as we fingered Emerson's pussy together. I want everything this man is willing to give me.

CHAPTER 22

I'VE WANTED THIS FOR so long. We took care of Emerson and she's resting in bed. I finally get to have Owen. I pull him to me and kiss him, thinking of all those times I wished I could kiss him. That wish has finally come true. I want to take it slow with Owen tonight. I don't want to make him uncomfortable. We discussed being together, but didn't go into detail. We're simply letting things happen naturally, I think, rather than giving a label to what's happening. I don't care if all I get is a kiss on the lips; I'm satisfied with that. If Owen's comfortable with more, then so am I.

He looks so fucking hot in his khaki slacks with his navy blue polo shirt hugging his tattooed biceps. While we're kissing, I tug on the bottom of his shirt, letting him know I want to see more of him, but that I'm okay if the answer is 'not yet.' His eyes meet mine, and he kisses me as he reaches up to grab the neck of his shirt and slides it over his shoulders. He doubles the favor and pulls my shirt off, too.

We're standing chest to chest and I can feel his dick through his slacks. Mine is constrained, too, but I don't want to rush this night. Owen's hands make their way to my waist, pulling my hips to his with such force that I instinctively grab his ass and press back against him. I want to touch every part of him, so I feel from his ass, up to his broad shoulders and down to his trim waist. I slide my hands up his arms, feeling his muscles that he works on in the gym with me. I've looked at these muscles for so long, wanting to touch them.

Owen takes my face in his hands and continues grazing his tongue over mine. His hands make their way down my neck, shoulders, and chest, and I can't keep mine from doing the same to him.

"Fuck, Drew. I can't believe this is happening," he rumbles.

"You? I've wanted you longer than I care to admit," I reply between kisses.

We turn our heads when we hear a sensual whisper from Emerson.

"I think I'm getting my energy back, but if you don't mind, I'll just lie here and watch the two of you get to know each other better."

Owen smiles at her. "You can watch all you want to, Baby." He turns his head back to me and draws his tongue from my neck to my shoulder.

"Drink your fill, Em. Let us know if you want to see something special," I tell her jokingly. To my surprise, she has a suggestion.

"I want to see Drew take you in his mouth, Owen." She says it without abandon, like she's thought about it many times before.

Looking at Owen, I see the heat in his eyes and I slowly move my hands to the button on his slacks. "We don't have to do this. Just tell me to stop and I will."

He unbuttons his pants for me and pulls the zipper down. I'll take that as meaning he wants this as much as I do. I move to my knees and he slides his fingers through my hair. Pulling his pants and boxers down until he steps out of them, I throw them to the side and I unabashedly enjoy the view in front of me.

My hands slide up his muscular thighs, and I take his dick in one hand, sliding the other around to caress his ass. Looking up at him while he looks down at me is the sexiest thing I think I've ever experienced.

"Have you ever done this before, Drew?" Owen murmurs.

"No," I tell him honestly. "I've only ever been with women. This is just as new for me as it is for you."

With a slightly shocked, yet hopeful, look on his face, he says, "I'm glad I'm your first."

I lick my lips and take him in my mouth the way I would want Emerson to do for me. I suck on him and relish the feeling of sliding my tongue around his head as I pump the base of his dick; the part that won't fit in my mouth.

I sense movement from the bed and realize Emerson has gotten up and is standing beside us, undressing. She lifts her sundress over her head and all we can see is her gorgeous curvy body in a sexy white lace bra and matching bikini underwear. She reaches around to unclasp her bra and, when it slides down her arms, I have to try hard not to come in my pants. Owen growls as she pulls her underwear down her sensuous legs and he can't help but reach over and feel her pussy. She moves closer to us and kisses Owen as he fingers her, which reminds me I'm pleasuring him. I continue licking his hard dick while she kisses him, playing with his tongue.

Owen grasps my hair and pulls my mouth away from his dick, saying, "Fuck, that feels so good, but with both of you on me, I'm going to lose it sooner than I want to." He takes my hands and pulls me to stand in front of him for another kiss.

"We need to give Owen a break," Emerson says to me.

Then I feel Owen's hands on my pants, unbuttoning them. I hear my zipper go down. Emerson is on her knees right beside me, sliding my pants down. I step out of my pants and Owen takes my dick in one hand, his wife's head in the other, and puts me in her mouth. When she closes her lips around me and sucks me into her warm mouth, I nearly come on the spot. I put one hand around Owen and one behind Emerson's head and enjoy the feel of her soft tongue.

Owen watches her as she gives me the best blow job of my life. "She's good, isn't she?"

"Oh fuck, yeah, Owen. Emerson, you're going to make me come, Baby, and I don't want to yet." I take her hands and pull her up in front of me so that we're all standing in front of each other. We take turns kissing one another while our hands explore each other's chests, and I commit the feel of Emerson's perfectly round boobs in my hands to memory in case this is all a glorious dream.

"Time for dessert," I tell Emerson as I lay her down on the edge of the bed. I get on my knees and she's at the perfect height for me to taste her. I slide my tongue through her pussy and she moans my name.

"Drew, that feels incredible."

"You taste incredible, Emerson." I lick every last inch of her between her legs, her lips, her clit, and the creases in her thighs, while Owen watches.

"My turn." He pushes me out of the way and it looks like I'm the one who has to watch now, but I'm enjoying the show. I sit beside her on the bed and massage her gorgeous breasts as I learn what she likes. Owen's known her longer and knows what she likes in bed, so when he circles his tongue around Emerson's clit and then sucks it into his mouth to make her scream, I tuck that tip away in my memories to try myself some other time.

"Owen, can I have Drew's dick in my pussy?" Emerson asks.

"Shit, Emerson, I never knew you were so..." Owen drifts off.

She finishes for him. "Sensual? Erotic? Provocative?"

"Yes. All of that," he groans into her pussy. "You don't have to ask. Baby, if you want Drew's dick in your pussy, you can have it. Drew?" He looks up at me.

I'm not going to pass this up. I've wanted this woman for so long I can't take it anymore. I reach for my wallet to grab a condom, but Emerson stops me.

"I have an IUD and we both get checked regularly for STDs. If you're clean, too, you don't need a condom."

"I'm clean," I mumble. "I'd love to feel you skin to skin. Are you sure? I haven't made love to anyone without a condom in over ten years." I look between her and Owen to see how they feel about this.

"I am absolutely sure," she says with a smile.

I take her in my arms as though she is the most precious thing on Earth, because she is, and I move her backwards up the bed to the pillows. I gently lay her down and crawl over her. Looking down at her, I tell her, "Emerson, my wish is finally coming true. I've wanted you so long, Baby."

"I'm yours," she says, as I take her mouth in a possessive kiss.

Owen is watching us and I can tell he wants to be a part of this. "Owen," I say, "slide your dick in her mouth while I put mine in her wet pussy." There is no hesitation before he takes a step over to the bed and slides her head to the edge where he can reach her. He caresses her beautiful face as he rubs his dick along her lips, and I touch my dick to her entrance. We all gaze at each other, and I ask her, "Are you ready?"

She licks her lips, looks at both of us with those exquisite eyes, and says, "Definitely. I want you both." At the same time, Owen and I slowly glide into Emerson, and all three of us express a groan of satisfaction from how good it feels to finally be together. Her pussy squeezes my dick tight and I can see her hollowed out cheeks as she sucks her husband. *Oh, how I want to be her husband, too.*

Owen and I find a steady rhythm, moving in and out of Emerson. The slick noises and the sexual moans only urge us all on. When Emerson reaches down to rub her fingers over her clit, I lose it. I hold on tight to her succulent thighs, pounding into her. My orgasm takes over my body and I come harder than I ever have before. Owen sees me spilling into her and it triggers his orgasm, too. He fists her hair and empties himself in her throat. As Owen and I are coming, Emerson's pussy starts to clench my dick as she rubs her clit and her second orgasm for the night takes over her body. She squeezes every last drop from me and swallows every drop from Owen. It is absolute heaven.

We all slowly float back down to Earth, and all we can do is smile at each other. I regretfully pull out of Emerson at the same time Owen does, and we get warm washcloths from the bathroom to clean ourselves up while Emerson catches her breath. Then, we pamper Emerson with fresh warm washcloths as we wipe her clean, too. The towels go in the laundry basket and we all climb into bed with Emerson in the middle on her back. Owen and I wrap our arms around her and hold on to each other, too. I drape my leg over hers and Owen does the same, so our feet are tangled together.

With a contented sigh, I tell her, "Emerson, you're ours. Forever."

Owen agrees. "And we're yours. We're never letting you go."

We fall asleep in each other's arms in complete ecstasy that I never knew existed until I met these two incredible people.

CHAPTER 23

Owen

WAKING UP NEXT TO Emerson and Drew is something I could get used to. Laying here looking at them, I realize how happy I've been over the last two days. Just being with them has made me—a somewhat grumpy guy who rarely smiles, says my wife—feel more free, hopeful, and complete. I decide to let them sleep in and go downstairs to make us all a nice breakfast before we go pick up the kids. If there's one thing I'm good at, it's cooking for a large crew, and breakfast is one of my specialties.

The bacon and sausage are sizzling while I'm finishing up the blueberry pancakes. The biscuits are already done and waiting on the table with all the fixin's. I just have to scramble up some eggs and breakfast will be ready.

"I knew I smelled something delicious," Emerson says as she walks up behind me and puts her arms around my waist. "Thank you for cooking breakfast."

Drew is right beside her and leans forward to kiss my neck. "Everything looks good, especially you two," Drew says.

"I hope you're hungry. I made a little bit of everything to eat this morning."

"I'm looking forward to it," Drew says, "and what we might get to eat after breakfast, too." He and Emerson pour glasses of orange juice for us and make their way to the table while I start plating the food.

During breakfast, we make plans to go to my parents to pick up the kids. It's a school night, after all, and we need to get them home by a decent time so they can wind down and get enough sleep.

"I figure I'll drive over to get the kids from my parents' house after breakfast. Do you guys want to go?"

"Sure," Emerson says, "just let me shower and get dressed first. Drew, do you want to go?"

"I wouldn't mind, but how do you think that will go? I've never met them before. How would you introduce me?"

"I'll just tell them you're my good friend, Drew. They've heard about you in the past, so they know of you," I tell him, taking his hand in mine. "I don't want to hide you, but we don't have to tell them we're in a relationship if we don't want to. What do you guys think?"

"That sounds good," Drew answers and Emerson nods her head. "We'll just play it by ear. It's fine with me if everyone knows we're together."

After breakfast, Emerson and Drew insist on cleaning up since I cooked, so I shower while they clean. When Emerson comes in to take her shower, I'm just finishing up and wrapping a towel around my waist. I can't help but watch while she undresses.

"Like what you see?" I tease her as she runs her hands over my bare chest. If anything, I'm the one admiring her curvy body. Even after decades of being together and her having kids, she's still the most gorgeous woman I know.

"Why, yes, I do. I'd like to see more." Emerson reaches for my towel and takes it off of me.

"What are you doing?" Oh, I know what she's doing, but there's no answer as she goes to her knees, sliding her hands down my body and wrapping her hand around my dick. She wraps her warm mouth around it and sucks me in as far as possible.

"Emerson, your mouth feels so good." I run my fingers through her hair while she licks from my base to the tip and all the way back. Her lips glide down my dick again until I can feel the back of her throat. I tighten my fingers in her hair just enough to put tension on it, and a sultry moan comes from her throat, sending shudders throughout my body. My head tilts back and I close my eyes until I hear movement at the bathroom door and Drew walks in.

"Mmm...delicious. I was hoping we would eat more after breakfast." Drew comes closer to me, wrapping his arms around me and kissing my lips. With his attention up top and Emerson's attention down below, I don't last long.

"Emerson, I'm going to come." I try to give her a chance to back away if she wants to, but she only sucks me harder and when I let go, she releases my dick and points it at her bare breasts. Looking down at this beautiful woman covered in my come, she is the sexiest thing I've ever seen. I offer her a hand getting to her feet and she kisses first me, then Drew. I'm spent, but Drew is just getting started. He takes his shirt off and tosses it into the laundry basket.

Drew kisses Emerson, pressing her against the bathroom wall, which makes him a little sticky, too. He lowers himself down and wraps her leg over his shoulder for easy access. "My turn, now," he says. He spreads her lips open with both hands and runs the flat of his tongue from her ass to her pussy. Just seeing him lick my wife—our wife—makes me hard again. I take her face in my hands and kiss her while he eats her out and all she can do is moan. I kiss her cheek, down her neck, her shoulder, and finally make my way to her nipples where I suck until they're hard peaks. I reach my hand around her back and caress her ass, then slide two fingers into her wet pussy while Drew is licking and sucking her clit. Her sexy moans only get louder.

"Fuck. Drew. Owen." she rasps. "I can't take much more."

Drew pulls his face away from her long enough to say, "Good. I want you to come all over both of us," and puts his mouth back on her pussy. Her eyes close and her head falls back while her body starts tensing up with the most luscious spasms. When she relaxes, Drew points her toward the shower.

"I'll get this one cleaned up and ready to go." He kisses me and climbs in the shower with her, where he proceeds to wash her hair and body. I just have to watch for a minute before I make myself leave them alone so I can get dressed to go pick up the kids.

***

Drew

"I'VE WANTED TO SHOWER with you ever since you let me undress you when I first moved in," I tell Emerson. "I like taking care of you, pampering you like a queen."

"I like it, too. It feels so good when you wash my hair and massage my scalp. Especially after what you just did. Mmm..."

"I'll get you all cleaned up and then we'll get dressed to leave. What a great way to start the day, huh?" I rinse the shampoo from her hair. I notice Owen is watching us and I don't mind at all. In fact, I kind of like it. I massage conditioner into Emerson's hair and rinse that out, then put some body wash on her pouf and clean her body. I suppose Owen decides he's seen enough and leaves me to our woman alone in the bathroom.

"It has been a great start to the day. Owen and I both had orgasms, but you haven't. I think it should be your turn," she says.

"Oh, really? It's okay. I don't have to..."

"I want to. How do you want it?" she says, looking up at me with those mesmerizing blue eyes. *Okay, if she's offering, I'm not turning her down.* I turn her around so her back is to me, slide my hands from her hips up her back and to her shoulders and gently push her forward so she's bending over. Her happy laugh tells me she likes my idea.

I draw my fingers between her legs, and she is still wet. Nudging my dick just barely at her pussy, I can feel her slight squeeze. I decide to tease her a little and push in slowly about an inch, then pull back out. After two more teases, Emerson is clearly ready for more because the next time I gently push in, she pushes herself back onto my dick so she's impaled on me.

"Aw, fuck, Emerson!"

"That's what you get for teasing me. Now fuck me. Please." And I do. I find a steady rhythm in and out that moves her entire body. I can see her breasts moving back and forth and watching my dick slide in and out of her pussy from behind is one of the best things I've ever seen.

"Emerson, I wish I could take a video from this angle so I can see this anytime I want."

"If it's this good every time, you can do it anytime you want. Harder, Drew." I fuck her pussy harder and faster until we're both panting and out of breath. She braces herself with one hand on the shower wall and reaches down to finger her clit with the other hand. She slides her fingers around my dick as I'm gliding in and out of her. I'm probably leaving bruises on her hips as tight as I'm gripping them, but I can't stop. She clenches around me and we both come at the same time. I'm sure Owen can hear us, no matter where he is in the house.

Emerson

These men have got me all twisted up. Our lives have changed so much lately that I need to talk to someone, and usually that person is Lauren. The guys are out washing their trucks before we go pick up the kids, so I decide now's a good time to call.

Dialing Lauren's number, I relax in the recliner while I'm waiting for her to pick up.

"Hey, Emerson!"

"Hey, Lauren, you busy?"

"Not really. I'm folding laundry, but I can chat with you on speaker while I do that. What's up?"

"You're not going to believe how my weekend has been going!"

"Let me guess, you won the lottery?" she asks.

"No, but pretty damn close to it. You know Owen's friend, Drew, has been coming over to our house a lot more lately, right? And he accidentally told me how he felt about me..."

"Mmmhmm...accidentally, my ass. I think he did it on purpose..." she interrupts me, laughing.

I interrupt her right back. "I don't think so. Whatever the case, he said it, and then when Grady moved out, Drew moved in to his room. We've all been getting along so well. Lauren, I have completely fallen in love with Drew."

"What about Owen?" she shrieks.

"That's the magical part. Of course, I still love Owen. Do you remember when Drew mentioned a while back that he had feelings for me and I told Owen about it because I didn't want to feel like I was hiding anything from him?"

"Yeah, I remember you told me a little about that. You wouldn't go into the details like I wanted you to, but..." she trails off.

"We all talked a lot about Drew's idea of having a triad relationship. Multiple times. I was hesitant at first because I didn't want to risk losing Owen, but over time, Owen has opened up to the idea. Lauren, this is it for us. I love them both so much I want to scream it to the world. The kids love them both. Keegan and Declan have both been spending time with Drew and I really think they look at him like a second dad. Grady even came over a few days ago to do some fishing with Drew on his day off."

"Aw, that's so sweet! I'm glad they're comfortable with your new relationship. That means a lot. I am so happy for you, Emerson. I'm still jealous, but happy, too," she laughs. "You deserve to be happy, and I can tell Owen and Drew love you."

We chat some more about Lamont, work, general girl stuff, and recent books we've read while I'm waiting for my guys. We have so much in common that it's easy to talk to Lauren, and I don't even realize how much time has gone by.

"Here they come. They must be done washing their trucks. We have to go pick up the kids after our weekend alone. It was so amazing. I'll see you at work tomorrow."

"And you'll share the details of this amazing weekend with your good friend?" she asks.

"Bye, Lauren..." I sing song as I click the end button.

CHAPTER 24

Emerson

We climb in Drew's truck and go to my in-laws' house to pick up the kids. Tomorrow's a school day, so we need to get back into our routine, but it sure has been one incredible weekend. I hope we have many more days together like the ones we've enjoyed lately.

Owen's parents come out on the porch when we pull up.

"Hey, how were the kids?" Owen asks, hugging his mom. The hugs continue all around.

"Oh, they were fine. They always are. We loved our weekend with them," his mom says. She looks at Drew and asks, "Who's this?"

"Mom, Dad, this is Drew. I've told you about him before."

"Oh, yes! I've heard lots about you, Drew!" She gives him a big momma bear hug and then Owen's dad shakes

Drew's hand. "It's so nice to finally meet you. Did y'all have a good weekend?"

"We did, Momma Callaghan. Thanks so much for keeping the kids," I tell her. "Are they ready to go?"

"I think so," Papa C says. "I think they're having withdrawals from their video games." The kids come out of the house with their bags and give us all hugs—goodbye hugs to Grandma and Grandpa and hello hugs to me, Owen, and Drew.

After saying our goodbyes, we're headed back home.

"Did you guys have a good time this weekend?" I ask Keegan and Declan.

"Yep! Grandpa took us out on the boat and we found a little beach," Declan says. "There was no one there, and I found some sharks' teeth!"

"That's awesome! You'll have to show them to me when we get home. How about you, Keegan? Did you enjoy your weekend?"

"Yeah, it was okay. I got a little tan on the boat." Keegan is getting to that age where it's not so cool to hang out with her grandparents.

"Well, I'm glad you guys had a good time. When we get home, get your chores and homework done before we have dinner. Everyone's home tonight for dinner, so I want to have a nice meal together."

While I'm cooking the kids' favorite meal, my family watches football in the living room. I can hear the laughter and bantering back and forth amongst them and it fills my heart. Declan is on Owen's side, rooting for his team. Keegan is cheering for the opposing team, which happens to be Drew's favorite team, just to irritate her dad.

"I'm with Dad. The Packers have got this one. We're on our own turf! We've gotta win!" Declan is so excited about their team winning.

Keegan isn't having it. "No way. No matter where they play, the Commanders have the best quarterback. I'm with Other Dad on this one. Commanders for the win!"

Drew raises an eyebrow and laughs. "Other Dad? That's what you're calling me now?"

"Sure, why not? You're like our second dad, right?" Declan says.

"You're always here for us and you do all the things Dad does. We do need to come up with a better name, though," Keegan says, thinking out loud.

Declan shouts, "I know! How about 'Big Poppa'?" and falls off the couch laughing so hard he can barely breathe.

"Riiiiight," Keegan replies. "I don't think so. How about Papa? Mom calls Dad's dad Papa C. We call him Grandpa. We can call Drew Papa."

Declan agrees with that. "Sounds good to me! What do you think, Papa?"

"I love it," Drew says.

"Ok, Papa and I say the Commanders are going to kick your butts!" Keegan quips.

I smile while I work in the kitchen because my kids are creating a special name for Drew. My heart is full. We've always been happy, even in the rough times, but Drew adds so much to our family. Yes, he does help around the house and makes life easier for me, but just his presence alone makes me happy. I can't imagine not having Drew in our life.

When dinner is finished and I've set the table, I call everyone in to eat together.

"How are things going at the station?" I ask Drew and Owen.

"Some of the new firefighters have turned out to be awesome, hardworking and really adding value to the crews," Drew says. "They're eager to learn the way we do things and get their training done."

"On the other hand, we've got a couple of duds, too," Owen adds. "A couple of them don't want to do anything around the station and think they can just hang out and play video games all day. That's not how it works."

"Yeah, they'll figure it out eventually. Hopefully, they learn that before they lose their jobs," I say, handing the plate with the steaks on it to Keegan.

"Nick's back to working on the floor. His knee healed up nicely, and he's back at 100%. No more desk duty for him." Owen says.

"I'm sure he's glad to get back into his regular routine," I mention as I pass the baked potatoes around the table. "Is he still dating Cate? How's that going?"

"He broke up with Cate," Drew says. "Nick said she wanted him to text her every time he went out on a call to let her know where he was and what he was doing. He tried to explain to her that we don't have time to text anyone when we arrive on scene because we're busy taking care of the fire or accident, whatever we're dealing with. She got mad, and they got into a fight about it."

"All I can do is shake my head. Sometimes people don't understand what you guys actually do," I tell them. "She reminds me of Lamont. Lauren said he constantly calls and texts her to confirm she is where she's supposed to be. She said he's changed dramatically since they got married, and not for the better. I was talking to her yesterday, and she told me about how he constantly criticizes her.

He's still rarely ever home, and when he is, he's acting strange. Last weekend, he just stayed outside in the backyard hanging around a bonfire he made and burning things. She asked if she and the kids could come hang out with him for some family time. You know, maybe make some s'mores or something, and he said he was busy cleaning up the yard and they shouldn't come out."

Owen frowns. "That's a little strange. Has he done that before?"

"Not that I know of," I tell him. "Lauren said he's been acting weird lately. I suggested they go to marriage counseling over the summer. I hope they do."

"Yeah, sounds like it might be a good idea for them," Owen says. "What's he do for a living again? Insurance or something?"

"Something like that. All I know is he works in an office from nine to five Monday through Friday," I answer. "I'd say it must be nice for Lauren to have her husband home every night, but she says he is always leaving for a meeting or something after work and on the weekends. His job wouldn't require him to have evening meetings or be on call. He won't tell her where he's been, either." Owen and Drew just shake their heads, which is all any of us can do.

"Declan and Keegan, tell us more about your weekend with Momma and Papa C. What did you guys do?" I ask the kids so they feel included in the conversation, too. Keegan tells us how Momma C taught her to bake pineapple upside down cake and Declan liked that part of the weekend because he got to eat it. Declan told us about fishing with Papa C off the boat and catching a small stingray that they threw back in the water.

After enjoying our family dinner, the kids offer to help me grade papers while Owen and Drew wash the dishes.

"I won't say no to that! Keegan, how about you check to see if the answers on these papers are correct according to this answer key? Declan, can you put a stamp on any papers that got an A or a B?"

With their help, we get the papers graded in no time and we all get cozy in the living room. The kids lounge in the chairs and I take my usual spot between Owen and Drew on the couch, only Drew sits much closer to me now than he did months ago. We watch a family movie until it's time for the kids to go to bed and then we head to bed ourselves to get some rest for the coming week.

Drew

"Hey there, Papa," Emerson purrs as I walk into my bedroom. She's sitting on the bed in her pajamas, reading a book and looking sexy as hell.

"You heard that, huh?" I reply with a shy grin. Owen walks up behind me, squeezing my shoulders.

"Yes, and I think it's so sweet. You know they love you," she says.

"She's right. The kids love you," Owen agrees.

"Yeah. I love them, too." I stand in front of Emerson. "They made me feel really great today. Being the most recent addition to the family, I have to admit that sometimes I feel like the fifth wheel. Like maybe I'm in the way and

I'm crowding your family space. I don't want to come into your lives and change everything."

Owen frowns as he stands beside me and takes one of my hands in his. "Drew, we love you. All of us. You are as much a part of this family as Emerson and I are. The kids look at you like another father figure, and I'm glad they do. You're a great dad to them."

"I have to agree," Emerson says as she takes my other hand. "The thing is, you did come into our lives and change everything...for the better. I wouldn't want to share this life with anyone else. You make us complete." She stands up and brushes her lips against mine gently; meaningfully. Then Owen takes my face in his strong hands and brushes his lips against mine, just like Emerson did.

Emerson begins taking off her pajamas as Owen and I watch her. When she is completely naked, she undresses me slowly, then does the same for Owen. She walks up to me and confidently puts her arms around my neck, presses her body to mine, and I soak in her intoxicating kiss. Owen steps behind Emerson, feeling her breasts and kissing her neck. Then she moves back just enough to slide her hand between us to massage my dick. She lowers her other hand to stroke my balls until I moan her name. Pushing me back onto the bed, she straddles me and slides down on me, her tight, wet pussy squeezing my dick.

"Emerson, you're making my dreams come true," I whisper in her ear.

Owen lays down beside me on the bed and watches her gorgeous body glide up and down on my dick. He doesn't touch me. He doesn't touch her. He just watches his beautiful wife fuck me. Then, he takes his dick in his hand and masturbates while he watches his wife please me, and

I've never been so fucking turned on in my life. My eyes squeeze shut when I cum hard inside of Emerson, and she keeps riding me until her orgasm makes her pussy clench my dick. Emerson and I watch Owen as he continues to jack off and cums all over his stomach.

After a quick shower where Owen and I wash Emerson and then ourselves, we crawl into bed together and lay there talking until we can't hold our eyes open anymore. As I drift off to sleep, I can feel their love surrounding me, and I think to myself that maybe I won't be alone for the rest of my life after all.

Chapter 25

Owen

DREW AND I ARE both on shift today at the station. We've got a long list of chores to do, so the entire crew has breakfast together and then we get started. Some of us work harder than others, but we get all the trucks cleaned and shined before noon and we head back in for some lunch. We get about half our chow down and suddenly, tones start wailing throughout the station and the dispatcher comes over the loudspeaker. Looks like the rest of the station chores will have to wait.

"Engine 41, Brush 42, Tanker 46, Medic 44: Please respond to a reported brush fire with flames showing at 6235 Waters Edge Circle. Be advised we have received several calls about this brush fire. Time out: 13:42."

We quickly step into our boots and turnout gear, and the trucks take off out of the bays with lights and sirens blaring.

Captain comes over the headset, telling everyone, "Be ready. It sounds like this one has something to it. If they've gotten several calls, it might be widespread."

We all nod a 10-4 and mentally prepare ourselves for what we might be working against when we get there. I know it must be big if they called all three of our trucks and the Medic for extra manpower.

We drive until the paved road turns into a gravel road only wide enough for one truck to pass and we can see the flames before we get to the address dispatch gave us. We pass a few small houses on stilts and I can see the road ends where the marsh begins.

Flames engulf the trees and tall grass, and orange embers float high above our heads. The billowing smoke is already hundreds of feet in the air, alerting anyone local that there's a large fire growing.

"Engine 41 is on scene. Captain Burrell in command. We have a brush fire approximately ten acres in size with flames showing. Fire is within approximately 500 feet of residential dwellings and moving closer."

"10-4. Engine 41 is 10-23 at 13:49," Dispatch relays. All the other apparatus mark on scene and then we hear directions from Burrell.

"Dispatch, please backfill our station and tone out for anyone from B shift that can possibly get here to bring another engine and tanker on scene. And call adjacent counties to help, too. We're gonna need 'em." Dispatch replies to Captain Burrell with a 10-4 and the radio shrieks tones once more, calling for backup.

Captain knows that with no fire hydrants out here in this rural part of town, tankers will play an important role in supplying us with water to fight this fire. He's smart to ask for help from neighboring counties to get enough trucks and manpower available because this fire is too much for us to handle alone.

"10-4. Dispatching additional personnel, engine, tanker, and backup at 13:51," she says. The intensity in the dispatcher's voice flows over the radio, and it shows she understands just how serious this fire is even though she can't see it.

"Let's get going, guys. We need to put some water on this thing before it reaches that house," Captain orders.

The scene is controlled chaos as we move quickly to unroll the hoses to get water flowing, all while making sure we're being safe and there are no bystanders that can get hurt. We already have a bunch of lifted pickup trucks and a couple of cars pulling up the road. People are already recording videos with their cell phones.

"Medic 44, 10-58 on incoming vehicles. Make sure they don't get too close," Captain instructs over the radio.

"10-4." Stathes drives the ambulance over to where the gravel meets the paved road to block any vehicles from coming any closer to the fire. People mean well, but they don't understand how much danger they're putting us and them in just by coming to see if they can help.

Dispatch comes over the radio. "Dispatch to Command: 10-72 at 14:05. Do you have an update?"

"Dispatch, we've got water on the fire, but we still need those other trucks. Are they 10-76?"

"Affirmative. Engine 26 and Tanker 23 are en route. ETA approximately three minutes."

"Tanker 46, stage close to the house and prepare to pump. Wet the ground around the house to prevent flames from spreading just in case it heads that way," Captain says into his radio. "I need two personnel from Tanker 46 to start cutting a fire line between the fire and that house so we don't lose it."

Captain Wiershen, Kounovsky, and Delgado from B shift arrive with another engine and have to drive around the bystanders and nearly in the marsh to get to the scene. Captain Burrell immediately assigns Wiershen and Kounovsky to an additional hose and puts Delgado on the fire line.

Right behind them, Ralbovsky, Montpetit, and Schultz roll up in the only other tanker we have at the station, and Burrell instructs them where to go.

Trucks and personnel from four surrounding counties converge to assist us. We have multiple hose lines on the fire and plenty of people cutting a line between the fire and the house, but the fire is gaining on us. Someone had to have used accelerants to start this fire; that's the only way it would be this out of control this quickly.

Burrell directs each new truck and its crew where to go and we surround the fire on all sides except the side that runs along the river. The billowing, gray smoke is thick and makes it difficult for us to breathe. Visibility is diminished, so we communicate over the radio when possible. I can't even begin to imagine how this fire is affecting the Chesapeake Bay Watershed.

Birds are flying away, squirrels are racing, and deer are leaping out of the forest of trees, all trying desperately to get away from the fire. The water quality will decline, erosion and flooding are more likely to happen, and there may even be toxic levels of Mercury released into the air and local waterways.

Our environment and our community will feel the effects of this fire for a long time. The flames are spreading inland, and if we don't get it under control soon, it's going to level that house.

Over my radio, I shout, "Captain, the flames jumped the fire line. They're getting close to that house."

"Damnit! You and Makris get everyone out of the house. You're the closest. And hurry! The wind is picking up. Two in, two out. Don't leave your partner," he reminds us. Then he adds, "Stathes and Muller, assist Callaghan and Makris at the residence. They're going in."

Drew and I immediately run to the house closest to the fire and bang on the front door while Stathes and Muller ready themselves at the truck.

"Firefighters!" I shout. "Fire is quickly approaching your home. We need to get you out." I don't wait for someone to open the door. I barge right in like I own the place and the first people I see, I start ushering out the door.

"How many people are in the house?" I ask a woman in her seventies.

In a frail voice, she starts to ramble. "Well, it's um...um...me and my husband. And my great grandson, Jason. He's 13. He's a tall fella, kinda cute, and loves playin' those verdio games. Oh, and my two cats, Eggplant and Taco. We were watchin' the Wheel of Fortune and..."

"Okay, thank you. We don't really need the details, ma'am. We need you and your husband to leave the house through the front door and talk to the firefighters in the front yard who are waiting for you. They'll direct you where to go so you're safe. We'll go find your great grandson."

"But my cats! Eggplant! Taco! Ya gotta save 'em!" she is screaming at the top of her little old lady lungs.

"Yes, ma'am, we'll do our best to find them after we find Jason. Now we need you to go outside," Drew tells them. She nods, but her husband looks pissed.

"I ain't goin' nowheres. You cain't tell me where to go or what ta do! These here is my properties," the husband shouts at us. I look over at Drew and I know he's thinking the same thing I am: this man smells like he's had way too much to drink tonight. If the fire gets to him, he'll surely go up in flames in a second.

Walking up to him, I say, "Yes, sir, we understand this is your house, but there is a fast-moving fire outside and it's getting closer and closer to your house. If you don't leave voluntarily, I'll have to pick you up and carry you outside."

"Dun't you put yer hands on me, boy!" I look at Drew and he nods. I hoist the old man over my shoulder just as I see fire licking the outside of the window pane on the far side of the living room. "We have to go now, sir. Your house is on fire!" I carry him, still fighting me, outside and his wife follows, still muttering on about her cats.

When they are safe outside, we take the attack line that Stathes and Muller have waiting for us and venture back into the house to look for Jason.

"Captain," Drew says over his radio, "We're going to need more help over here. B side of the house is fully engulfed and spreading." Captain sends over two crews to hose down the side of the house closest to the fire, which is already caught in the flames. We now have over forty men and women from five different fire stations battling this blaze over an area of approximately fourteen acres.

"Drew, stick with me, man. We gotta find this kid." I head in and he follows me. We search all the rooms on the first floor and can't find anyone—neither Jason nor the damn cats. We head up the stairs, shouting his name. I hear coughing, so I turn right and there he is, laying on the floor.

"Got him." I take my respirator off and put it up to his face so he can inhale clean oxygen. His heartbeat is slow and he is barely moving. Once he's had a few breaths of air, I put my mask back on, haul him over my shoulder, and we turn around so Drew can lead us back down the stairs and out of the house.

The fire has spread to the ceiling, and smoke has filled at least eighty percent of the house. I hear Captain talking over the radio.

"Hurry up and get your asses out of there!" He speaks to dispatch next. "10-72 dispatch, fire has spread to a residential dwelling. Two-story house is twenty percent involved."

We're carefully descending the stairs when I hear a loud crack amidst the roaring flames and all three of us start falling. We fall for what seems like forever in slow motion, through the stairs that have opened up like a sinkhole in the Earth. I land on my right side with the kid face-down on top of me. Drew lands face-down on the hardwood floor and he's not moving.

Black smoke is billowing all around us, and flames are crawling toward us. With what little energy I have, I try to shake Drew and shout his name, but there's no response. I reach for the radio on my shoulder and use the last ounce of strength I have to push the button. *He can't die.*

"Mayday! Mayday! Firefighter down," I try to scream over my radio. It only comes out as a ragged whisper.

"Makris is down. I repeat, Makris is down!" *I can't let him die.* The flames are still roaring all around us as scorching darkness envelops all of my senses.

Chapter 26

Emerson

"Hello?" No one ever calls my cell during school hours, so I answer it in case it's important. The kids are working in groups on a STEAM project, so they probably won't even notice.

"Mrs. Callaghan?"

"Yes, this is she."

"This is Sylvia, a nurse at Hicks Evans Memorial Hospital. I'm sorry to inform you that we have your husband here in the emergency department. We were hoping you could come in."

"What?! Of course! I'll be right there." I immediately call the front office to let them know I need someone to cover my class for the rest of the day and why. I'm throwing the bare necessities in my purse just as Principal Jenkins walks in.

"Go ahead. I'll take care of your kids. Give us an update when you can."

"Thank you, I will. Lesson plans are on my desk. I have to go."

In my car and backing out of the parking space within minutes, it feels like forever before I get to the hospital. What adds even more time is having to park on the other side of the parking lot and walk what must be a mile to get inside.

A whoosh of the automatic door gushes past my ears as I walk in. I'm met with sharp clinical lights, dusty plastic plants, and the smell of antiseptic as I search for the nurses' station.

"I'm Emerson Callaghan. You all called to tell me my husband is here." The nurse directs me to Emergency Room 117, but finding it is like navigating a maze, even with the nurse's directions that barely registered in my head. When I finally find it and walk into his room, my heart drops.

Owen is in a hospital bed with bandages on his neck and his arm in a sling. An oxygen mask is positioned over his mouth and nose; his hoarse snore telling me he is sound asleep.

Captain Wiershen enters the gloomy room cautiously.

I turn and stare at her, speechless and teary-eyed.

"Whenever you're ready, I can fill you in on what happened at the call and the doctor can answer any medical questions you may have."

"Thank you. Yes, please fill me in. What happened?"

"Owen and his partner were coming down the stairs in a structure fire when the stairway suddenly collapsed beneath them. Another team went in to rescue them and found them both unconscious on the first floor, along with the child they saved. Owen will need to take some time to recover, but he is going to be fine."

"Thank you so much. Do you know if Drew Makris is here? Is he okay?"

"He is here. Down the hall in room 126. He didn't have any family listed for us to call."

"We're his family."

"Okay, then, we'll make a note of that at the nurses' station. You probably know, then, that Drew was Owen's partner in the fire tonight. Drew suffered some injuries in the fall as well. The doctor can give you more information about him. They saved a teenager's life today.

"If you have any questions regarding Drew or Owen, please let me know. Here's my contact info in case I'm not here when you need me." She hands me her business card and leaves me to wrap my head around the fact that both of the men I love are in the emergency department.

Sitting in the chair beside Owen's bed, I take his hand in mine to kiss his fingers. "I hope you're going to be okay, Owen. I don't know what I'd do without you." My eyes are focused on the cuts and bruises on his face as I hear gentle footsteps behind me.

"Mrs. Callaghan?" A low voice asks.

"Yes."

"I'm Dr. Roberts. Along with the nurses, I've been helping to take care of your husband while he's been here. Do you feel ready to discuss his situation? If you need some time, I can come back later."

"Of course, yes. Please tell me what's going on. He's going to be okay, right?" I'm sure he can see the concern in my eyes as I hope for positive news.

"Yes, Owen will make a full recovery. He suffered burns to his neck and strained his right arm when he fell. Owen has some damage to his lungs from the smoke and we're treating him for extreme exhaustion. He needs all the sleep he can get, but you're welcome to visit as long as you'd like.

I want you to know he helped save a young man's life today. The young man has some minor injuries, but he's going to be just fine thanks to your husband and his partner."

I'm finally able to take in some air, and a frail sob escapes my lips. "Oh, thank you so much, Dr. Roberts. What about Drew Makris in room 126? Do you have an update about him?"

"I'm sorry, are you family of his? He did not list anyone on his emergency paperwork with the fire station, so we had no one to call."

"Yes, I'm his...I'm his family. Please tell me how he is."

With a dubious look, he reluctantly goes on. "When the stairs below Drew and Owen collapsed, Drew fell and landed in a prone position. This caused damage to his face as well as a broken wrist and a broken radius and ulna all on his left arm. He has torn ligaments in his left knee.

Like Owen, he also has some signs of extreme exhaustion and has some first and second-degree burns on his neck that should heal in time. We expect him to make a full recovery after physical therapy. He's sedated right now to encourage him to rest."

"Is it possible for me to see him? They're like brothers. Is there any way they can share a room so I can be with both of them?"

"Sure, of course. Drew is in a double room with no other patient, so we can move Owen over to his room as soon as the nurses are available. Please call for me if you need anything or have questions. I'll give you some time to process all this information." Dr. Roberts shakes my hand, nods, and exits the same way he came in.

Sitting in this dreary space, I am relieved that Owen and Drew will be okay. Their job is a dangerous one, so it goes without saying that they are risking their health and lives when they respond to a call at work. They do it anyway because that's the kind of men they are; compassionate, altruistic, and brave.

Our community benefits tremendously from people like them. However, their spouses have a lot to agonize about until their firefighter walks back through their front door, safe and sound at home.

Owen's hand twitches in mine, and he begins to stir. As his eyes flutter open to figure out where he is, he tests his voice.

"Em...Emerson? What happened?" He clears his throat.

"You're going to be fine, Honey, but you and Drew were hurt in a structure fire. You're in the hospital."

"Drew. Where is he?" He coughs. "Is he okay? I tried to..."

"Shhh...he's okay, Owen. He's in another room. He suffered some injuries, too, but he's going to be fine. The nurses will be here soon to take you to see him."

"Oh, God, thank you. We fell...and I tried to wake him, but he didn't respond." Owen draws in a ragged gasp. "I could barely move...It was hard to breathe...I fell with the boy on top of me...oh no! The boy! Is he okay?"

"The doctor said he's going to be fine. He's got some scratches and bruises, too, but you and Drew saved his life." Owen's entire body relaxes with the knowledge that Drew and the teenager will be okay.

We sit in silence in the dark, each engrossed in our own thoughts. My mind veers down a treacherous road that shows me how horrible my life might be if I lose either Owen or Drew, and I have to pull myself back to the here and now. Thinking that way will get me nowhere and I need to be strong for my men.

"Owen, are you ready to be transferred now?" A nurse walks in and begins preparing Owen and his bed for the short trip down the hall to be with Drew.

"Yes, thank you. I need to see Drew, please."

"Honey, I'll get out of the nurses' way so they can move you and I'll meet you in Drew's room."

Leaving a kiss on Owen's clammy forehead, I set off to find Drew's room. I need to see him with my own eyes to make sure he's okay, but I need to make a couple of phone calls first.

***

"Momma C? It's Emerson."

"Hey, Sweetie. How's everything goin' hun?"

"Well, everything is fine, but I need you to do me a favor."

"Of course, anything. You name it."

"Like I said, everything is fine, but Owen and Drew worked a structure fire today and they are both in the hospital with some injuries."

She gasps. I know this is one of her worst fears as the mother of a firefighter.

"They're both going to be okay. Please let Papa C know, too. I'm at the hospital now with them. The kids should be getting home from school soon. Could you stay at the house with them for the night? I need to be here with their dads."

"Of course I will! You're sure they're going to be okay?"

"Yes. The doctor said they should fully recover. They both suffered from exhaustion, smoke inhalation, and they have some cuts and bruises, but they will be fine. I just left Owen, and I'm on my way to see Drew. It would be a big help if you could be with the kids at home, so I don't have to worry about them."

"I'm on my way there now. You call me right away if you need anything."

"Yes ma'am, and thank you." I disconnect the call and then realize, in my haste... *I said dads. Oh no, we haven't really explained our relationship to Owen's parents. Maybe she didn't catch what I said? I can't worry about that right now.*

I make a quick call to let Grady know what happened, and he says he's on his way to the hospital. Then I send a text update to Principal Jenkins.

Hi Mrs. Jenkins. Just wanted to let you know Owen is doing okay. He has some minor injuries, but he will have a full recovery. I will not be able to work the rest of this week. I'll update you more asap.

Thank you, Emerson. I'm praying for you and your family. Let us know what we can do to help. I'll schedule a substitute for you for the rest of the week.

After contacting everyone I needed to, I peek into Drew's room and make my way in.

Laying in his bed with an IV in his arm, an oxygen mask covering most of his handsome face, and wires connected to several places on his body, Drew looks run down and weak. I kiss his forehead and sit in the square chair on the other side of his bed, so I'm not in the way when the nurses bring Owen in.

Drew is sleeping soundly and I figure that must be due to the sedation the doctors gave him to help him sleep. His left wrist and arm are in a sling and there is a splint on his left leg. I rest my hand on his right leg just to be able to touch him and my thoughts run away again with What Ifs.

What if they hadn't stayed together in the structure fire? What if the roof collapsed on them instead of just the stairway? What if the other firefighter team hadn't gotten to them in time?

I feel so terrible that Drew had no one listed on his emergency contacts for the hospital to call. We need to fix that right away. Owen, the kids, and I are his family. We're here for him, no matter what. We love him unconditionally.

***

THE NURSES ROLL OWEN'S bed in and get him situated again with his IV and wires, and then leave to let him rest. I move my chair to the space in between Owen's and Drew's beds so I can sit next to both of them.

Owen looks at me with red, irritated eyes and asks, "Where are the kids?" It's just like him to ask about the kids. He is such a great dad.

"I talked to your mom. She's going to the house to be with them tonight so I can be here with you guys. I also called Grady to let him know what happened. He's on his way here right now."

Right then, Momma C walks in the room. "Actually, I'm here right now. The kids wanted to stop by and see you for themselves. I did, too." Momma C says, walking in the door and gently hugging Owen. She's followed by Keegan, Declan, and Papa C.

"Hey guys. You didn't have to come all the way up here," Owen tells her.

"Yes, I did. My grandchildren wanted to see for themselves that their dads were okay. So I brought them. Here, Emerson, I brought you a change of clothes and toiletries you might need for the night, too."

"What would we do without you, Momma C?" I ask as I hug her. I noticed how she casually threw in there the word dads—plural. She knows. And she seems to be okay with it. Just to be sure...

"Momma C, about our relationship..." I start, but she cuts me off, grabbing my hand in one of hers and patting it with the other.

"I completely understand, and there's no need to talk about it right now. You just need to make sure your guys get better." My guys. She really does seem to be okay with it.

"They're going to be just fine," I say, mostly for the kids' benefit.

"Has the doctor mentioned when you'll be able to come home?" Owen's dad asks.

"Not yet," I tell them, "but that's on my list of questions to ask once he makes his rounds again. As you can see, Owen is tired, but awake. They've sedated Drew to help him rest. His injuries were a little worse than Owen's and recovery will take a little more time and effort for him."

"Well, we'll all be here to help both of you with whatever you need," Papa C tells Owen.

"Thanks, Dad."

"Alright kids, give hugs all around and let's get you back home for some dinner." Papa C is not one to hang around and chat. Once they've said their goodbyes, they leave and Dr. Roberts comes in.

CHAPTER 27

Emerson

"HEY THERE, MR. CALLAGHAN, Mrs. Callaghan. I'm glad to see we could get you moved to the double room. I just wanted to stop by to do a quick check on you and answer any questions you might have."

While Dr. Roberts is listening to Owen's heart rate and lungs, I ask him my most pressing question. "When will Owen and Drew be able to leave the hospital?"

"Owen is doing pretty well, but I'd like to keep him for observation for at least one night, if that's ok with you, Owen." Owen nods. "Drew's sedation will wear off this evening and, depending on how he's doing, he may be able to go home tomorrow, too. We'll have to wait and see."

"Thanks, Doc," Owen tells him. "We appreciate your help."

"Of course. That's what we're here for. You just make sure you don't get hurt next time you're in a structure fire. I don't want to see you in here again anytime soon. Your vitals are looking good. Your lungs sound a little rough and we'll give you some medicine to help you with that. I want you sleeping as much as you can tonight." Dr. Roberts records Owen's vitals on his medical chart, repeats the same procedure with Drew, and moves on to his next patient.

Owen and I hold hands for a few moments in comfortable silence. His hand is cold in mine, so I find another blanket in the closet and cover him with it, tucking in his feet so they're warm. Kissing him on his lips, I tell him, "I'm so glad you're both okay. I don't know what I'd do if I lost either of you."

"Oh honey, don't worry. You won't lose us. We're always careful."

"Yes, but accidents happen. In your line of work, they happen more often than normal. I'll never get used to you guys being in dangerous situations."

"Neither will I," Grady says as he walks in the room. "How ya' feelin' Dad?"

"Oh, I'm alright, Grady. Just a few bumps and bruises. Drew here has it worse than me. We'll be okay, though."

"I was worried. The fire was all over the news. What happened?"

Owen goes on to tell Grady about the structure fire, how they ended up upstairs, and how they ended up downstairs. Grady takes it all in and just lets Owen get it all off his chest. He needs to talk about it. That's one thing that will help these guys get through this scary situation. I just listen to them talk as Owen conveys the timeline of the fire and Grady responds with oohs and aahs as the story unfolds.

Eventually, the story is told and Grady's concern is eased, so he leaves to let his dad get some much needed rest.

While Owen and Drew are resting, my phone vibrates and the caller ID shows Lauren's name. I step out of their room and find a seat in the vacant family waiting room.

"Hello?"

"Hey Emerson, how are you guys doing? I saw the fire on the news. Was Owen there?" Lauren sounds worried.

"Yes, he was there. He and Drew were upstairs in the house when the stairway collapsed."

"Oh no! How are they? Are they okay?"

"They're a little worse for the wear. They're both suffering from smoke inhalation, exhaustion, and burns on their necks where their gear didn't quite cover them. Owen strained his right arm, but Drew took the brunt of the fall. He has some facial damage, his left wrist and arm are broken, and he tore some ligaments in his left knee."

"What can I do to help? Do you need me to take care of the kids?"

"Thank you, but no. Owen's parents are with them. They're doing fine."

"How are you doing with all of this? The doctors and nurses are taking care of the guys. What about you?" she asks.

"I'll be fine as long as they're fine. I'm worried about them, Lauren. I don't know what I'd do if I lost one or both of them. Why do they have to have such a fucking dangerous job?"

"Aw, you know they're helpers, Sweetie. It's in their nature to run into the building when everyone else is running away from the fire. It sounds like they'll be okay. Have the doctors talked to you?"

"Yes. He said they'll be able to go home in a day or two and they'll be fine in time. This was a close call, and it really scared me, Lauren."

"I know. I know you love Owen. You've been with him for years. And now you've gotten close to Drew, considering what you told me about last weekend."

"I love Owen and Drew. Both of them. I need them to be okay."

"They will be, Emerson. They will be."

Drew

The slight smell of antiseptic fills my nose and I can hear beeping in the distance. I feel like I'm waking up from a long sleep with sluggish limbs and hazy memories. It feels as though my left arm and leg are immovable, but even if I could, I'm not sure I'd have the energy to move them. The back of my neck feels like it's burning, but my lungs...my lungs feel like they're on fire. Voices seem far away, but I think I can hear Emerson's sweet words.

"I'm so glad you're both okay. I don't know what I'd do if I lost either of you."

As I listen to the voices, I slowly start to remember the fire.

The brush fire spread to the house.

We found the boy.

Came downstairs.

Then it all went blank.

I try to pry open my eyes, but they're heavy. I'll rest for a minute and...

***

COMING TO, I TRY again to open my eyes and a thin slice of my surroundings comes into view. I try to clear my throat of the cobwebs that are choking me and barely a sound comes out.

"Did you hear that?" Emerson asks.

"Drew?" She comes to my side and I can feel her presence. It felt like I didn't completely exist and when she got closer, she made me almost whole. *Where is Owen?*

I struggle to open my eyes and I can see her standing above me, peering into my face. She takes my hand and kisses my fingers. "Hi, Honey. How are you feeling?"

All I can do is groan.

"It's okay, take your time. The doctors and nurses gave you some sedation medicine to help you sleep. It'll take some time for it to wear off."

"Owen?" I rasp out.

"Owen is fine. He's right here in the room with us. He has some injuries he's recovering from, too, but you'll both be just fine."

"What happened? All I remember is grabbing the kid and coming back downstairs."

"The stairs collapsed underneath you and Owen. You both fell to the first floor. Your left arm is broken and your left leg is injured." *That explains why I can't move them.* "You suffered some smoke inhalation and exhaustion. The doctor said we'll see how you're recovering tonight and he may let you go home tomorrow if you improve enough."

"Okay. Thanks, Em." She leans forward and gives me a gentle kiss on my dry lips. She sits beside me on the bed, holding my hand, and the world dims again.

Owen

I understand why I have to be here in the hospital, but I can't wait to get into my own bed. I've been doing nothing but sleeping or recounting the drama to family and friends who have visited. I want to go home and take a steaming hot shower. No one can relax in the hospital.

"Mr. Callaghan," Dr. Roberts says as he enters our room, "how are you feeling? I just wanted to check on you one more time before I head home for the evening."

"Doing okay, Doc. Wish I could go home, though."

"Let's get through the night and see how things go. Your vitals are looking good, so assuming nothing changes, you can go home in the morning. If you need anything, please let the nurses or doctor on duty tonight know. They'll take good care of you."

"Thanks, Doc," I say as we shake hands and he looks over at Drew.

"Please let Drew know I stopped by to check on him, too. I'm glad to see he's sleeping." Emerson and I both nod and he continues on to his next patient.

Sitting beside me on the bed, Emerson gently kisses my cheek. "Can I get you anything before you go to sleep for the night, honey?"

"You. I need you. Could you lay here with me for a little while?"

"Of course." She lays her head on my chest and I can feel her heartbeat against my side. Her arm wraps around my waist and I encircle her in mine, savoring her warm body.

***

Morning light filters in through the edges of the curtains and I realize Emerson and I fell asleep wrapped in each other's arms. She yawns and looks up at me.

"How did you sleep, Owen?"

"Best sleep a guy could get in one of these hospital beds." I wink at her to let her know she's the reason I got any sleep at all. She smiles and her eyes travel down my body to where the sheet is tented in my lap. "Any chance you want to help a guy out with that?"

She laughs and shakes her head. "I can tell you're feeling better. Let's get you home and settled and we'll see about getting you some help."

Emerson helps me to the bathroom and then back to bed to eat the breakfast they've brought in. I'm actually hungry today, so I dive right in to the scrambled eggs and yogurt as Emerson helps Drew with his breakfast. It's not easy doing anything with only one good hand.

After breakfast, Nurse Sylvia comes in to give me my last breathing treatment and do one last check of my vitals. Then she leaves and comes back with discharge paperwork and explains to Emerson and me the procedure I have to follow in order to continue recovering well.

"Drew, I'm taking Owen home. Once I get him settled in, I'll come back to spend the day with you. Try to get some sleep, okay?" She kisses his forehead, and he nods his weary head.

On the ride home, Emerson fills me in on how the kids have been doing with all of this. Apparently, they haven't let it impact their school work much at all and my parents are keeping things running at the house. I am so thankful that we have extended family around to help in times like these.

"I also need to tell you about something else concerning your parents. I don't know if you remember or were even awake when they visited you, but they know about our triad with Drew."

"They do?"

"Yeah. When I called your mom to let her know you were in the hospital, I accidentally said, 'I need to be here with their dads' when I was talking about you and Drew. I didn't know at the time if she caught what I said, but later when they visited you, she let me know she did. She seems perfectly fine with it. I'm sure they will have some questions, but she encouraged me to just take care of you guys and make sure you both were okay."

"That sounds like her. I'm glad you let me know. And I'm sort of glad my parents know. I never intended to hide it from them, or anyone for that matter, but I suppose the idea of it never came up. I'm glad it's out in the open."

"Me, too. I'll let Drew know when he comes home from the hospital. For now, let's get you in the house and comfortable."

***

"IT FEELS SO GOOD to be in my own bed," I tell Emerson as she's helping me get situated.

"What else can I bring you? I want to make sure you're set up with everything you need for the night, since I'm going back to hang out with Drew. You've got some snacks and the remote, and your mom will bring you dinner when it's ready. Anything else you want?"

"You. Can I have you?"

"Not right now. Eventually, yes. Let that be your incentive for healing quickly and getting back to normal. We don't need to strain your lungs anymore than they already have been."

"Okay, but just know I don't like it. Thanks for getting me situated, Honey. Go and be with Drew. He needs you right now."

She leans over, places her smooth hands on my jaw, and gives me a kiss before she heads back downstairs. Looks like I'm Netflix-n-chillin' by myself tonight.

Chapter 28

Drew

"YOU HAVE TO LET me go home today. I've been in here two nights and I can't get any sleep." It's as if there's a revolving door attached to my room, with nurses and orderlies going in and out on the regular.

Dr. Roberts remains stoic as he replies, "Your vitals are stable and your lungs are looking better. You could do the nebulized therapy at home. I'm just worried about your lack of mobility. You won't be able to walk up stairs."

"I'll sleep in the living room. I promise. Give me a wheelchair. I need to get home."

"Alright. Let me go finish my rounds and I'll see what I can do." He saunters out of the imaginary revolving door and in walks Emerson.

"I'm so glad you're here. You're a sight for sore eyes. How's Owen doing?" I ask her.

Emerson leans down to hug me and I soak in her calming scent that is uniquely her. She has been staying with me as much as possible here at the hospital, but checking in on Owen and the kids on a regular basis, too.

"Everyone is doing well. Owen is up and moving around, so he and I will both be able to help you when we get you home. I'm here with you for the night."

"Good, I'm glad Owen's doing alright. You may not have to stay tonight," I tell her, and she looks at me curiously. "The doctor just left and said he'd try to get me discharged today. I can't wait to get back home."

***

EMERSON FILLED ME IN on everything happening at home as we drove away from the hospital. I don't know what we'd do without extended family to help with the kids. They've been able to continue school and not miss a beat as we've been going through this ordeal. In fact, Momma C says that Keegan has really stepped up and helped out around the house. I'm so proud of her.

Emerson also filled me in on how Owen's parents found out we're in a relationship, and I'm so relieved that they're comfortable with it. It means a lot to me that they approve of me being a part of their life. Owen's parents have gone home to rest up after playing house with their grandkids, so now it's just me, Owen, Emerson, and the kids at the house.

Emerson's got me set up on the couch in the living room and she, Owen, and Keegan are doting on me like momma birds with a baby. I'll take it, though. I'm just glad to be home from the hospital. Looking back, there was a time when this was just a friend's home, not my home. This family made me dream of having my own family and my own home. Here I am, living my dream.

Declan has been entertaining me with video games and even played a couple of hands of cards with me to keep me company.

"Ha! I win again!" he teases as Emerson sets a sandwich and a drink on the table beside me. I wink at her to say thanks.

"Only because I'm injured, Dude," I quip.

Declan stops and faces me, eyebrows knitted together with a frown.

"Papa, I'm glad you're okay. I was really worried about you." He leans over and hugs me so tight that the shattered pieces of my heart mend together a little bit more.

Hugging him just as tightly, I tell him, "I'm fine, Declan. Don't you worry about me. I'm safe now and I'm so blessed that you and the rest of our family are taking care of me. I'll be back to my old self in no time."

"Want to play another game?" he says, changing the subject.

"Nah, I'm getting tired of losing to you, man. How about you go practice soccer while it's still light outside? I think I'll eat my lunch and then get some rest."

"Okay. I need to practice my dribbling and shooting, anyway. Let me know if you need anything." He's really stepped up to the plate. I couldn't have asked for a better family to love and cherish as much as I do these people that have absorbed me into their lives.

***

Owen

AFTER GETTING DINNER GOING in the crock pot, I amble into the living room to check on Drew. He's laid up on the couch, staring at the ceiling.

"You look lost in thought. What's on your mind?" I ask him, sitting down in the chair across from him.

Looking over at me with thoughtful eyes, he says, "Nothing. Just thinking."

"Thinking about what? Talk to me. Maybe I can help."

He sits up on the couch as best he can and motions for me to come over.

Gazing into my eyes, he says, "We've come so far and so much has happened in such a short amount of time. I was thinking about how lucky I am to have you and our family. There was a time when I felt alone. Even when we talked about me moving in, I wasn't sure if it would work or if I would fit in to an already established family. I didn't want to mess things up for you, your wife, and your kids."

Slipping my fingers through his, I tell him adamantly, "You haven't. Drew, you make us a better family. You complete our family. You bring so much joy and happiness to us that I can't even put it into words. I can't imagine my life without you in it now. Emerson is not just my wife. She's yours, too. Grady, Keegan, and Declan think of you like a dad. They're your kids, too. For life."

Looking into his gorgeous blue eyes, I lean forward and let my lips graze his; a gentle, slow kiss that I hope says what's in my heart. Sliding my hand to his cheek, I kiss him again, running my tongue along his bottom lip. He opens for me and our kiss quickly turns from caring to passionate. Before things go too far, and get too hard, I pull back and look at him confidently.

"Drew? What do you think about making this permanent and official?"

"What do you mean?" He squints his eyes at me the way he does when he's trying to figure me out.

"I mean, let's make our relationship as official as we can. What do you think about the two of us asking Emerson to marry us? We'll have a ceremony with an officiant and everything. Our life doesn't consist of my family plus a friend. I want you to be my husband and Emerson's husband equally. I want Emerson to be your wife, too."

I get off the couch and down on one knee in front of him to prove I'm serious. Taking both of his hands in mine, I ask fervently, "Will you marry me, Drew?" I raise my eyebrows in anticipation of his answer.

He scans my face and his gaze finally lands on mine when his one good hand slides up to my cheek. He kisses me deeply and with so much emotion, it chokes me up inside.

"Nothing would make me happier than to marry you, Owen."

"Sorry I don't have a ring," I joke, and he laughs.

"That's okay. We'll get one for Emerson."

***

AFTER DINNER, WHILE EMERSON is in the shower, Drew and I make our way out to the back deck to talk with Keegan and Declan. We dial up Grady and put him on speakerphone so he can listen in, too.

We like to do things as a family unit, so we want to include them in this momentous decision. We all sit on the back deck just to make sure Emerson doesn't walk in on us and spoil everything.

After sitting down on the other end of the bench I'm sitting on and pushing his wheelchair out of the way, Drew begins.

"Keegan, Declan, and Grady. Dad and I want to talk to you about something."

"Sure, Papa. What's up?" Keegan asks. Declan eagerly awaits our response, too.

"I would like to make Drew an official part of our family, so I've asked him to marry me," I inform them. "Of course, he said yes, because I'm a catch, as we all know." This earns me a couple of grunts, a laugh, and a jab to the arm.

Continuing, I say, "We would like to ask your mom to marry us both, of course. How would you guys feel about that?"

Declan speaks up first. "Are you going to have a wedding and stuff?"

I tell him yes.

He asks, "Will we have to dress up?"

I tell him yes. He groans.

"Declan," Keegan says, "They're asking how we feel about the three of them getting married. Now's not the time to worry about if you have to wear a tuxedo or not." She turns to Drew and me, and says, "Dad, Papa, I would love for you to ask Mom to marry you both. And I'd love to help plan the wedding. I bet Declan would agree." She nudges Declan when he doesn't speak up.

"Yeah, that's cool. Just don't make me dress up." Everyone laughs and Drew and I hug our kids.

Emerson

After my shower, I walk around the house in search of my family, only to find everyone gathered outside on the back deck. I'm half-tempted to enjoy some peace and quiet alone, but decide to head outside. When I walk through the door, they all stop talking and glance at me. *Suspicious.*

"What? You were talking about me, weren't you?" They all immediately start shaking their heads.

"Nope. We were talking about soccer," Drew says quickly.

"Just figuring out how we can all get to Declan's game on Saturday morning," Owen adds. "We might have to take two vehicles."

"Yeah, we probably will," I agree. I sit down between Owen and Drew on the bench and take both their hands in mine. "Why are you guys all outside?"

"It's such a nice night. Who would want to be inside? It's warm, the stars are shining, and we have our whole family here together," Drew says. "There's nowhere else I'd rather be." He squeezes my hand, kisses my cheek, and looks up at the sky dreamily.

We enjoy the night air, the crickets chirping, and each other's company until the bugs start to annoy us.

Smacking at a mosquito, I say, "Kiddos, I think we better head to bed before the bugs carry us off somewhere. It's a school night." Luckily, they don't argue tonight and they start their nighttime routines.

Drew, Owen, and I complete our nighttime ritual, too, including locking the house up, turning off all the lights, and tucking the kids in to bed. Drew rolls around in his wheelchair as best he can, helping us, and then awkwardly moves himself to the couch—his temporary bedroom.

"The kids will be asleep in no time. You guys want to watch a movie with me?" Drew asks.

"I have a better idea. How about you come upstairs and we all get comfy in your bed?" Owen suggests.

"How am I going to do that? I can't get up the stairs. You guys go on without me," Drew mutters.

Owen responds by walking over to him and pulling Drew up by his waist.

"Hey, what are you..." Drew exclaims as Owen hefts Drew over his shoulder into a firefighter carry and strides up the stairs.

"You coming, Emerson?" Owen asks me.

Oh, I hope so. I'm right on their heels.

Chapter 29

Emerson

When Owen sits Drew down on the bed, Drew says, "I promised the doctor I wouldn't walk up the stairs."

"You didn't. I carried you," Owen replies with a kiss. "I miss you in our bed. Now, let's get comfortable."

And with that, Owen sits beside Drew on the bed and they begin to undress each other as I sit on the bed and watch like some sort of voyeur. When they're finished and I can see all of their glorious bodies, except for what's hidden by Drew's arm cast and knee brace, Owen pulls me over to stand in front of them and they repeat the process with me.

"I've been waiting to get both of you alone and in bed again," Owen says as he pulls my nipple into his mouth.

"I don't know how much I can...uh...participate tonight," Drew mumbles from beside him as leans forward and pulls my other nipple into his mouth.

Owen reaches over and fists Drew's dick, saying, "You don't have to worry. We'll take care of you."

I hold them close, running one hand through Drew's hair and caressing Owen's head with the other as they kiss, suck, and lick my breasts. Owen continues to massage Drew's dick until he's moaning against my skin. Drew slips his fingers through the folds of my pussy to find me wet and waiting for him. Owen slides his other hand around my back and fingers me from behind.

"Fuck, I've missed this. You. Both of you," Drew groans.

"Drew, Honey, lay back on the bed," I tell him. Owen helps him move back to lean against the headboard so his legs are spread out on the bed.

Being careful of his knee brace, I kneel between Drew's legs and slide my hands up his muscular calves and thighs, massaging where I can. When my hands reach his dick, I lean forward on my knees with my ass in the air to lick a drop of precum away and suck him into my mouth. His fingers on his arm without the cast slide through my hair and grasp just tight enough to make me even wetter than I already am. He's hard, huge, and he feels so good in my mouth.

I feel the bed dip down and Owen's hands glide from my feet, up my calves, and to my thighs. He caresses me, rubbing his thumbs over my ass cheeks and slowly circling that little pucker between my cheeks. When he slides his finger in just a little, it makes me moan onto Drew's cock, which makes Drew moan.

"You like that, Baby?" Owen asks.

All I can manage to say is, "MmmHmm."

"Owen, whatever you're doing, she likes it. Emerson's sucking my dick like she never has before. She's sucking me deep and her moaning like that is going to make me come down her throat."

"Drew, you should see me finger our woman's ass. It's fucking sexy as hell. I'm two knuckles deep and she's squeezing me so tight."

Drew replies, "It must look hot if it's making you pump your dick like that." I look over my shoulder to see Owen on his knees behind me with one hand fisting his cock like he wants to fuck me.

"It is, and God, I need to be inside one of you. Now." He gently pulls his finger out of my ass, saying, "Baby, we're going to try that again with some lube next time." Then he crawls closer to me on the bed and runs the head of his dick along my pussy and ass, teasing me.

"Owen, you need to stop teasing me and fuck me right now. I want both of your cocks inside of me." And before I can get the words out, he shoves his big dick in my pussy so deep I can almost feel it in my chest. He pushes into me, shoving me down onto Drew's dick and making all of us cry out. Drew watches me suck him while Owen pounds into me from behind and can't help telling us what he's thinking.

"I've never seen anything sexier than the two of you tonight. Owen, yes, fuck her. Fuck our woman's pussy until she squeezes you and comes all over your dick. Emerson, does Owen's hard dick feel good inside of you, Baby?"

"Fuck yes," I say, barely able to form words.

It's Owen's turn for dirty talk. "Yeah, that's right, Emerson, suck his huge cock until he comes down your throat. I'm going to keep fucking your tight, wet pussy until you make Drew explode in your mouth." As he says those words, Drew does exactly that. Hot come fills my mouth and I swallow as much as I can.

Owen doesn't let up and continues plunging into me. When Drew finishes, Owen slides out of me, and turns me over beside Drew on my back. I throw my head back and gulp in air like I just breached the surface of the ocean.

Owen hovers over me on his knees and gets right back to work, shoving into me again and finding a steady, deep rhythm that makes my toes curl. Drew reaches over to finger the folds of my pussy as Owen's dick slides in and out of me. When Drew focuses on my clit, I lose all control and start to see sparkles in my peripheral vision.

"Damn, Emerson, your pussy is clenching me tight. I can feel you spasming around me. I'm going to come inside of you, Baby," Owen says, and he does. He explodes into me while Drew continues to finger my clit and I dissolve into a puddle as my eyes close and darkness surrounds me.

***

Bright light shines in my eyes, so I drag my arm up to cover them. I feel a massive arm encircle my waist and hold me tight.

"Why is it so bright in here?" I grumble.

"It's morning, Sweetheart," Drew says. Last night starts to come back to me.

"Owen is already downstairs getting the kids ready for school. Are you going in to work today? Or did we wear you out last night?" Drew smirks and rubs his nose against mine.

"Yes, you guys wore me out. That was one of the most intense orgasms I've ever had. But, also yes, I have to go in to work. I've taken so much time off this year that I can't miss any of the last week."

I climb out of bed and get dressed, thankful that Mrs. Jenkins decided to let the teachers dress down and wear jeans these last five days. I throw on my nicest comfy jeans and my t-shirt that says, "Ain't no tired like teacher tired," and head to the bathroom to finish getting ready.

Before I head downstairs, I hug and kiss Drew. "I love you honey," I say, and he repeats it back to me.

Downstairs, Owen has a lunch packed for me and all my teacher bags ready and waiting by the door.

"I can't imagine why," he winks, "but I know you're running a bit behind this morning, so I made you a coffee and a biscuit to go. Need anything else?"

I shake my head, telling him, "No. I couldn't possibly ask for anything else. The two of you have given me everything I need or could ever want. I love you both." I hug and kiss him, I'm on my way to work.

***

In the teacher's lounge, Lauren sits beside me and begins unpacking her lunch bag.

"How's everything going at home? How are the guys? I still can't get over that horrible fire," Lauren says.

"They're doing surprisingly well, thank goodness. Owen is almost back to his old self and Drew just has a little ways to go. He still has his arm cast and a knee brace, but he's able to get around the house using his wheelchair. Soon, he'll be able to use a knee walker and get around more easily. Once he finishes physical therapy for his knee and gets his arm cast off in a few weeks, he'll be as good as new. Even with all the things we're dealing with at home, I am so happy with my guys."

"Yeah, the three of you make a good team. I'm a little jealous!" Lauren says.

"How are things with you? How are Lamont and the kids doing?"

"The kids are fine. Happy that school is almost over for the year. Don't even ask about Lamont," she says, rolling her eyes.

"Oh no, what happened?" I ask.

She takes a deep breath and says, "I just don't know what to do. He's not the same man I married. He used to be so kind and loving. Now, he won't let me leave the house without knowing exactly where I'll be and who I'll be with. If I'm on the phone, he has to know who I'm talking to. I noticed the changes had been taking place slowly, but looking back over time, I can see a huge difference in him between now and when we got married."

"Have you talked to him about it?"

"Yes. Well, as much as one person can talk, anyway. I've tried talking until I'm blue in the face. Lamont won't talk to me. Says it's his right as my husband to know where I am and what I'm doing. I don't know how long I can deal with this. We're going to have to have a major discussion this summer. I'm just trying to get through the end of the school year and hopefully we can work on our marriage more this summer."

Reaching over to hug her, I say, "I'm so sorry, Lauren. It sounds like we've both been going through hard times. We can get through this, though. We're tough. We'll support each other and everything will be fine."

She wraps her arms around me in return, saying, "I sure as hell hope so."

"After today, we've got four more days, and then we'll be free to focus on our own personal well-being. Maybe you and Lamont can meet with a marriage counselor together this summer. If he won't agree to that, you could still talk with a therapist to help yourself through these changes you're seeing."

"I think that's a great idea. I'll have to call around...as soon as we make it through this week. The students are off their rockers!" Lauren laughs.

"You've got that right!" Glinnie, a 1st grade teacher, sits down with us to begin her lunch period. "Hey girls, how you doin'? Makin' it through our last week?"

"Just barely," I tell her. "Only a few more days. We can do this."

"Yes, we can," she says between bites of her sandwich. "I have to say, Emerson, I've noticed you look so happy lately. What's changed? You almost seem like a different person. You seem so relaxed and cheerful lately."

"Oh, I don't know, Glinnie," I say, winking at Lauren, "I guess I've just got some good people on my team these days."

"Well, I'm glad. You deserve it, girl," she says with a smile.

We chat a little more and finish up our lunch so we can pick up our students on time and get back to our classrooms. The countdown for summer is on.

Chapter 30

Emerson

Driving home from work, I can't help but think of Lauren and how lucky I am to have not one, but two wonderful men to love and support me and our kids. I hope she and Lamont can get through this rough patch in their relationship.

After pulling into the driveway, I grab my teacher bags, my drink, and my empty lunch bag and make my way into the house. Dinner, along with my beautiful family, is waiting for me when I get home. We eat as a family, one of those precious nights where we're all home together. We've had our rough patches, but we got through them with love, patience, and understanding. Our home is filled with a forever kind of love that I will do my damnedest to preserve and protect for the rest of my life.

***

"Ahhhh... Saturday. We finally made it to summer!" I say excitedly to the kids. They're just as happy as I am that school's out and we can relax. I'll still have training and professional development to do this summer for work, but I plan on taking it easy and enjoying time with my family. It makes up for all the extra hours I have to work during the school year.

"Are we going on vacation this summer?" Declan asks.

"Of course, dweeb, we always do," Keegan tells him.

"Keegan, be nice to your brother. Don't start bickering or it'll be a long, aggravating summer."

The rumble of Owen's truck comes up the driveway, letting us know he's home from his shift at work. The shifts aren't as long these days because quite a few of the new hires made it through the academy, so there's much less mandatory overtime now. Owen and Drew have been working their regular schedule, so they're each only gone for two days at a time now.

Drew's shifts overlap with Owen's, so every few days, they are both home. Of course, every few days, they're both at work, and I enjoy having those days, too. It's nice to have some time for just me and the kids, or just me if the kids are visiting with Momma and Papa C.

"What are you guys up to?" Owen says as he comes in the door from work.

"The kids are writing down their ideas of what they want to do this summer—sort of like a summer bucket list. Maybe I should make one, too," I say.

"You should. I bet I know one thing you'd put on it."

"What's that?"

"How would you like to go have a picnic? The whole family," he adds.

"I would love that. Want to head to the beach where we went last time?" I ask. That was such a gorgeous day and I'll never forget that was the day Drew and Owen kissed for the first time. It was the beginning of our family taking a big chance by following our hearts.

"That sounds perfect. I think I hear Drew pulling up the driveway now. We'll get everything ready, watch Declan's soccer game, and then we'll head out for a day at the beach." Owen pulls me in for a bear hug and kisses me long enough that the kids get grossed out.

"Eww...get a room..." Declan says. He and Keegan head off down the hallway to their bedrooms, and Owen and I make our way to the kitchen to get lunch together for everyone.

Drew joins us in the kitchen and drops a kiss on my lips, then Owen's. We fill Drew in on the plans for the day, and while we're making sandwiches in the kitchen, we hear the TV announcing breaking news, so we all rush to see what they've discovered.

"This just in: Police have arrested Coruscate Turner for her alleged involvement in the recent brush fires plaguing the community that resulted in the complete loss of several acres of land, a family home and their two pet cats, as well as an indeterminate amount of resources from local and surrounding county emergency personnel and operations departments.

"Prosecutors are charging the suspect with first degree arson, a felony punishable in Virginia by at least five years, or potentially life, in prison. Similar cases in Virginia history have resulted in six-figure fines to cover the damages done and expenses incurred by intentionally setting fires to occupied buildings and the surrounding landscape. Environmentalists state the effects of the recent brush fires will be felt for years to come. More on this story tonight at six."

We're all staring at the TV in awe and slowly begin to come to our senses. Looking around the living room, the relief is palpable as I take in Drew's and Owen's faces. I rush to them, wrap my arms around them both, and thank the powers that be for an end to this terrible wreckage that has impacted so many in our community.

Drew is the first one to speak.

"Why does that name sound familiar?"

"Coruscate? Isn't that Cate, the girl Nick broke up with?" I ask.

"I think you're right." Owen says. "There can't be too many people with that name around here. It's an unusual name."

"I wonder if he knows she's been arrested?" I wonder aloud.

"No idea, but I suppose we'll find out more on our next shift," Drew says.

***

AFTER DECLAN'S TEAM WINS their soccer game, we all meet out in the parking lot to hear Declan's play-by-play of the two goals he scored, along with all the other details from the field.

When Declan finishes his animated replay, Drew says, "I'm getting hungry for lunch. Why don't I take the kids in my truck and you guys can go in Owen's truck to the beach?"

"Sounds good to me. We'll meet you there," Owen says.

After piling into the trucks, we head toward the river for a family day. The puffy clouds in the sky are picture perfect and the wind is blowing just enough to make for a breezy, comfortable day.

"There's a lot of traffic today," Owen mentions.

"Yeah," I agree. "There was a great turnout for the game today, plus it's the beginning of summer, so everyone is out and about on the weekend. I'm not even sure I see Drew's truck anymore. Do you see him?"

"Nah, but it's okay. We both know how to get there and where we're going. We'll just meet up at the picnic table," he tells me.

We park and gather the picnic basket and blanket, and walk over to our favorite picnic table. Drew and the kids aren't there yet, so we begin setting up lunch. By the time the tablecloth is spread out and the food is ready to be opened and plated, we still haven't seen them.

"Think we should call them?" I ask.

"Nah, let's walk down the boardwalk and see if they're down by the beach," he suggests.

Owen grabs my hand, and we walk over to our spot overlooking the beach. Sure enough, Drew is there, waiting for us, just peering out at the horizon. He turns around just as we walk up to him and pulls me in for a hug.

"Hey, there," he says. "I was wondering if you guys got lost."

"Nah, just held up in traffic. We got the picnic ready," Owen tells him.

"That's great," Drew says with his arm still around my shoulder, giving Owen a fist bump.

Drew looks at us affectionately and says, "Emerson, Owen, I love you both more than I could ever express in words." He takes each of our hands and continues as the sun shines down on us through soft clouds and the wind blows gently around us.

"I cannot imagine my life without both of you in it. Before I came to Virginia and met you, Owen, I was a broken mess, barely getting through each day. You became my best friend and helped start my healing process. The more I got to know you, Emerson, the better friends we became. Until one day, I realized that I didn't want to be only friends with either of you.

"Emerson, I love what a beautiful soul you have. You care for others around you and you are the best mother to your children. Owen, your strength and resilience inspire me every day. I respect and admire you both to no end. I want to be able to say that you're mine, and I'm yours, for every day of my life."

Owen reaches for my hand, and the two of them lead me to the edge of the overlook, where I can see our three children standing on the beach, waving at us.

I smile at our kids since my hands are threaded with Drew's and Owen's hands. Then I notice the writing in the sand.

WILL YOU MARRY US?

I look at Owen and Drew, and they both smoothly kneel in front of me on one knee. These handsome men hold the most beautiful ring in a black velvet box between them. The round diamond in the middle is the largest of the three-stone diamond ring. A second and third diamond protect it on each side. On each side of those three diamonds are a cluster of three birthstones—one for each of our children. Drawing in a breath, my hands cover my mouth and my eyes tear up.

Owen and Drew look up at me from their kneeling position and Owen says, "You are the most amazing woman we've ever met. Our family of six is complete now. We want to have a unity ceremony to show everyone that we love each other and will be with each other forever."

"We love you, Emerson, and we want to spend the rest of our lives with you," Drew says. "I want to take care of you when you're not well, feed you donuts and brownies, and fall asleep with you and Owen every night."

"I want to come home from work to you and Drew after each shift," Owen continues, "knowing you've taken care of each other and the kids while I was gone. I want to be there for both of you and wake up to both of you every morning that I can."

"Will you do us the honor of being our wife for the rest of our lives?" Owen asks.

"Will you marry us?" Drew asks.

Looking from Owen and Drew over to my kids, who are giving me thumbs up signals, and looking back at my guys again, I wipe away a tear that's escaped down my cheek.

"Yes! Of course! Nothing in this world would make me happier than to be married to both of you for the rest of my life. I love you both."

They stand and embrace me as the kids walk over to us and join in. I take in the view, my beautiful family, and the exquisite ring Drew is sliding on my ring finger, and I can't help but think... *What more could anyone ask for?*

The End

Epilogue

Emerson
One Year Later

KEEGAN HELPED US PLAN the most beautiful beach-side wedding ceremony over the summer. Since we'd all been married once before, and since Declan couldn't stand to wear anything formal, we went with a casual theme. Khaki shorts and a white, collared, short-sleeved shirt looked handsome on Owen, Drew, their Best Man, Grady, and their Groomsman, Declan. Blue flowing dresses looked elegant on my Maid of Honor, Keegan, and my bridesmaid, Lauren.

Lined up along the beach, Drew and Owen waited for me with handsome smiles as Papa Callaghan walked me down the aisle and Momma Callaghan dabbed at tears on her cheeks as she sat in the rented white chairs with blue and white bows. Surrounded by family and friends we love, the officiant led us through an unforgettable ceremony, uniting the three of us as one before we each read our own vows to one another. Even though we can't officially all get married in Virginia, we know in our hearts that we belong to one another.

One of my favorite pictures from the ceremony hangs on the wall at the entrance to our home and shows all six of us pouring our share of sand into one large glass vase, validating our commitment to one another and showing that our whole is made up of many smaller parts that cannot be dismantled easily. That vase of sand is the centerpiece of our living room and I'm happy to share its story with anyone who will listen. How we became Mr., Mr., and Mrs. Callaghan-Makris and kids is my favorite story.

"Bye, Mom, Dad, and Papa. Mrs. Jackson and Liam are here to pick me up for the football game," Keegan says as Liam knocks on the door.

"Hey Liam. I didn't know you were going to come inside," she says quietly to the young man at the door.

"I wanted to introduce myself to your parents," he says. He looks at us standing in the living room. "Hi, Mrs. Callaghan-Makris. I'm Liam Jackson, Keegan's boyfriend," he says, coming forward to shake my hand.

Then he turns to Owen and Drew. "Hello, Mr. and Mr. Callaghan-Makris, it's nice to finally meet you," Liam says, shaking their hands as well.

"Good to meet you, too, Liam," Drew says. "What are your plans for the day?"

"Well, sir, we'd like to grab a bite to eat before the game. Then, the game starts at 5:00pm and it should be over by 9:00pm at the latest. Keegan is going to sit in the bleachers with my mom and watch the game, if that's okay with you all. Then we'll bring her right home."

Drew and Owen nod their approval and Owen says, "Have fun, guys."

Liam opens the door for Keegan and follows her to the car where he opens the door and takes her hand to help her get in.

"I like that guy much better than the last one," Drew says as Declan comes bursting in the back door with his soccer ball.

"Me, too," Owen says. "All done with practice, Captain Declan?"

"Yep, I'm ready for tomorrow. Is it okay if I ride with Grady and his girlfriend to my soccer game tomorrow? They said they would stop by and pick me up if it's okay and Coach Alex said it's a good idea for the team captain to get there early."

"Sure, hun, that's fine. We'll just meet you there," I tell him. "For now, I'm going to go make dinner. What are you guys going to do?"

"Want to go fishing off the dock?" Declan asks his dads.

"Sure," they agree simultaneously, and they all head out to the garage to get their fishing equipment while I prepare dinner.

This has become our normal weekend routine during the school year. I cook on Saturdays and one of the guys cooks on Sundays so I can get my lesson planning done. Owen and Drew are both home more often now that they've hired new firefighters and overtime has dwindled. Drew, Owen, and the kids help around the house so much now that we have plenty of time to do family things on the weekends. Because of their work schedules, we're still not all home every night, but we cherish the nights we are all together and go with the flow the rest of the time.

After cooking and setting the table, I call the guys in to eat and Declan entertains us with his lively rendition of a Mr. Beast episode he watched recently.

"Mr. Beast built over one hundred homes for people who didn't have any homes!" he tells us excitedly.

"I thought Mr. Beast made gaming videos?" Owen says.

"Yeah, he does, but he makes so much money as a YouTuber that he donates a lot of it and does nice things for people around the world. I want to do the same thing when I'm on the US National Men's Soccer Team."

"That's a very nice thing to do, Declan," I tell him, glad that he's at least thinking about the future.

The guys insist on cleaning up after dinner while I take my shower and then Declan heads off to shower, too. Once Owen and Drew join us in the living room after getting ready for bed, we watch a movie until Keegan gets home. Liam opens the door for her to let her in and then walks back to his mom's car.

"How was the game, Sweetheart?" Drew asks.

"It was great. Liam's team won! I had the best time hanging out with his mom. She's cool. I'm going to head up to shower and go to bed."

"Sounds like a plan. We're doing the same. We have Declan's soccer game in the morning," I remind her.

"Goodnight, Keegan. Goodnight, Declan," Owen says to them.

"Awww, why do I have to go to bed now?" Declan whines. Some things never change.

***

"Mrs. Callaghan-Makris, are you ready for bed?" Drew asks, walking into the bedroom the three of us have shared since we got married and closing the door behind him.

"Yes, sirs, I am," I tell him and Owen.

"Good girl," he and Owen say at the same time, and a wave of sensation flows over my entire body. They stalk toward me where I'm standing beside the bed, taking their shirts off as they go, and enclose me in their arms, with Drew in front of me and Owen behind me. Drew places his hands on either side of my face and tilts my face up to meet his so he can leave feather-light kisses along my jaw and cheeks as Owen grips my waist in his strong hands and kisses his way down my neck to my shoulder.

"Drew, do you think you're ready tonight?" Owen asks him.

"Yeah. Let's give it a try," he says, taking off my pajama shirt.

"What are you guys up to?" I ask.

"Drew and I have been up to no good, Emerson. Has he told you?" Owen asks, pulling down my pajama shorts.

"No, but I'd love to hear all about it," I reply. A shiver runs down my naked body.

"Drew told me he wants to try something new with us, so we've been playing with anal plugs. Yet another first we get to experience together."

I can't believe what I'm hearing. There was a time when I wasn't sure if Drew and Owen would ever kiss, much less make love with each other.

"I'm intrigued," I say. "Owen, you're ready for that?"

"Yes. It's been on my mind for a while and I can't wait to try. It sure as hell turned me on when we were trying out different sized plugs. I think we're ready." Owen and Drew remove their sweatpants at the same time. Feeling their bodies against mine, their warm muscles against my skin, is such a seductive feeling.

Drew turns me to face Owen and Owen delivers a rough kiss that makes my stomach clench as my arms wrap around his neck. From behind me, Drew slides his hands over my body and Owen's, touching and kissing both of us anywhere he can. He cups Owen's hard dick and glides it between my legs and through my slick folds.

"Emerson," Drew says, "Lay down on the bed for me."

I do as he says, while Owen kisses Drew the same rough way he kissed me. My eyes are drawn to their dicks rubbing against each other. It's so fucking sexy. Releasing Drew from the kiss, Owen climbs on the bed and crawls toward me. He leans down to lick my pussy and an erotic moan escapes my lips.

"That's right, Owen," Drew says. "Lick my wife's pussy. Make her feel good." Owen does exactly that as Drew crawls on the bed beside me to play with my nipples. He teases them to hard peaks and then slides his hand down to my pussy where Owen is sucking my clit. He slides two fingers into me, pumping in and out like he wants to fuck me with his dick, and it's enough to send me over the edge. I gasp as my orgasm takes over me with Drew's fingers inside me and Owen sucking my clit. Tremors ripple over my body from my head to my toes and every muscle in my body seizes as my orgasm ebbs and flows. My body eventually relaxes and Owen crawls up my body to kiss me.

He leans over to kiss Drew and their kiss grows intense with growls and small nips of each other's lips.

"I want you, Drew," Owen moans and moves backward so Drew can take his place.

Drew climbs on top of me, one leg on either side of me, kissing me as his dick instinctively slides into my pussy a little bit. I hear Owen open the bedside table drawer. Drew gasps a little when the cold lube touches his skin. Then I see Owen put the bottle of lube down and rub his hands over Drew's back, massaging as he rubs himself against Drew's ass.

"You ready, Emerson?" Drew asks me.

"You ready, Drew?" Owen asks with a smirk.

"Hell yes," we both answer. Drew pushes his dick into my sensitive pussy, both of us moaning until he's as deep as he can go. He stays there, not moving, his eyes locked on mine.

I can feel Owen push him forward a little bit as he begins to enter him from behind.

"Oh my God, that feels so good, Owen. Emerson, don't move, Baby, or this is going to be over sooner than we want it to be." He leans forward and rests his forehead on mine, taking deep breaths.

"You have no idea how hot this is, guys," I tell them. Owen continues pushing into Drew, which pushes him further into me.

"Drew, I'm in. All the way, handsome. You can breathe now." Drew takes a deep breath and then Owen starts moving. A small push forward pushes Drew into me. A small withdrawal moves Drew away from me. Owen finds a steady rhythm in and out and soon all three of us are groaning and whispering each other's names.

"I'm so glad I accidentally slipped up and told you I wanted you, Emerson," Drew says. "The sensation of being with both of you together...This is absolute Heaven. I love you both." He can't hold back anymore. He lets go and his orgasm overtakes him.

"Oh my God, you're squeezing my dick, Drew. It's even better than I imagined it would be. I love you both so much." Owen's head falls back as he gives in to his orgasm.

Seeing these handsome two men on top of me enjoying each other and me, it is the best sexual experience I've ever been a part of and I want so much more of it. My second orgasm rips through my body and my eyes close in pure pleasure. When I gain my senses back, I tell my guys, "I love you. Now and forever."

Epilogue 2

Owen

AT THE STATION ON our next shift, Drew and I are
sitting beside each other in the kitchen eating dinner as
Nick Papciak walks in. I take my hand off Drew's thigh
because we're not supposed to date anyone we work
with. I'm hoping it doesn't get out to everyone that
we're married now, but news travels fast in fire stations.
Showing any type of public display of affection in the
station, like rubbing up on my husband's thick thigh,
is going to get us in trouble. I don't know how we're
going to keep it a secret, but I'll do whatever I have to.
I love working where I am, but if I have to move to a
different shift or even a different station, I will. I'll do
anything I can to keep Drew in our lives. He, Emerson,
and I have been so happy for so long. I'm not going to
give it up.

Papciak lays all his ingredients out on the counter and starts cooking his food, then mumbles, "So, I guess you guys heard they arrested someone for those fires."

Drew and I look at each other. "Yeah, man. It was that girl you were dating, right? Cate?" I ask.

"Yeah. I can't believe I never saw it. I mean, she always wanted to know about the calls we were on and what we were doing. She constantly asked how things were going with the arsonist and if the police had found any evidence. I can't believe I didn't put it together."

"Where is she now?" Drew asks.

"She's in a minimum security psych ward so she can get the help she needs, but also be under the watch of a police officer at all times. You know, she called me from the psych ward. She gets one phone call a day," he adds while he's finishing up cooking his dinner.

"What did she want? Why did she call you?" I wonder aloud.

"She told me she's talking to a therapist every day. They told her she's what's known as a Pyrophiliac. It's someone who is compelled to set fires to satisfy psycho-sexual cravings. She asked me if there was any chance of us getting back together."

"What'd you say to that, man?" Drew says.

"I told her no. We broke up before she was ever arrested for this shit. As much as I hate to hurt her when she's already in a mess of trouble as it is, I don't want to lead her on and make her think I'm waiting for her until she gets released."

"Good thing," I tell him.

"I just should've seen it, though, you know? Cate was always wanting to go to the station or be around the equipment. She even applied for a job as a firefighter, you guys! She's not trained to be a firefighter. Cate went around pouring gasoline all over the trees and marsh just to set fires and make us run on all those calls. She told the police that she'd go hide and stick around to watch us put out the fires. That's how they found her. She'd been watching that house fire where y'all got hurt and someone saw her hiding behind the shed. I feel bad that I brought her around the station, guys."

"Don't beat yourself up, Nick," I tell him. "It's not your fault. Like you said, there's something going on with Cate and she needs therapy. They'll help her where she is."

"You know Cate isn't even her real name? I found out when the police wanted to question me about our relationship. She changed her name from Kelly to Coruscate. Do you know what that means? Coruscate means to sparkle, flare, or burn. As in fire. She renamed herself after fire." He puts his head in his hands as he sits down at the table with his dinner plate.

"It'll be a long time before I date anyone else," he continues. "That's for sure. I need some time to get over all of that."

Roderick Muller walks in and sits down with a pizza he ordered. "Get over what?"

"Cate and all that mess she caused, setting the fires," he answers.

"Well, at least she was hot," Muller says. "She was hot every time she started one of those fires and stuck around to watch," he says, laughing.

"You think you're so funny, Muller. If you had stayed for that cookout we had at my house way back when, you'd have seen how strange she was," I tell him. "Why did you leave early that day, anyway?"

"None of your business, man. And hey, Nick, I'm just trying to lighten the mood. Forget about it," Muller says in a mafia voice. "It's over now. I bet you're dating someone else within the next coupla months."

Drew

After a busy day at the station, we all make our way upstairs to our racks. We've had a few calls today, plus some in-person drills. I'm wore out. Climbing the stairs, I think about how lucky I am that I have Owen, Emerson, and the kids in my life. Come Hell or high water, I'm going to do whatever I have to do to keep them in my life.

I suppress a moan as Owen's fine ass is climbing the stairs in front of me. I'm the last person in the stairwell, so I take advantage of no one being behind me and I pinch his ass. He turns around with wide eyes that say *you better watch it.* If anyone found out we were together, we'd be in for it.

Once we get upstairs, everyone goes their separate ways. Papciak and Stathes grab their shower stuff out of their lockers. Owen and Muller go to their racks to make up their beds for the night, and I head into my bunk room to change my clothes. Captain Burrell must still be in his office.

I already showered, so I toss my shirt and pants into the laundry and pull on a pair of shorts to sleep in. When I glance at the picture I have taped to the inside of my personal cabinet, it reminds me of how fortunate I am. It's a family picture of all six of us and it makes me so proud and grateful every night I'm on shift. I have to make sure I lock my cabinet when I leave, so no one else sees it.

Closing the cabinet, I fall onto the bed and flip through the channels on my TV, hoping to find something interesting to occupy myself until I can fall asleep, and settle on Criminal Minds.

After that episode goes off, I hear a knock on my door. I open it to find Owen standing there in just his sleep shorts, broad chest and tattoos bare in all their glory, which makes my dick twitch. The rest of the hallway looks bare and dark, as though everyone else has gone to bed.

"What's up?" I ask Owen, standing in the doorway.

"Can't sleep. What about you?"

"Same."

Owen looks left, and then right, and when he sees no one in the hallway, he leans forward to kiss me. It's a quick kiss at first, like he just wants to say goodnight, but then as though he can't help it—neither can I—he slips his hand up to my cheek and kisses me again with a slow, lingering kiss that heats me up from the inside out.

When we hear matching gasps a few feet away in the hallway, we abruptly stop and look around. We just barely glimpse Papciak disappearing from the showers into his bedroom and Muller's door closes at about the same time.

Eyes huge with worry, Owen and I look back at each other.

"Oh, shit," we manage to say together.

***

THERE'S MORE TO COME!

This series will include five additional books so that everyone at the Riverfront Fire Department will get their happily ever after.

In the next book, Nick Papciak and Roderick Muller become heroes and protect their secrets in *Igniting the Heart*.

Keep in touch for more sweet and spicy polyamorous stories!

Acknowledgements

I appreciate you.

I want to take time to acknowledge all the emergency service families out there. This life is hard. I see you. I see your efforts, your struggles, and your wins. Thank you for providing emergency services to your community.

If you're not an emergency service family, thank you to those of you who support the brave people who are. You are all heroes.

Many thanks to Belle, Brittni, Mesa, Leslie, Stacey, A.L., Alissa, Nathalie, and Alyssa for lending your wisdom and support in this crazy book-writing adventure.

Thank you to my gorgeous ARC Readers and all of my friends who have supported me and inspired me to follow my dreams.

Most importantly, thank you to my fellow bibliophiles. I hope you have enjoyed reading this book as much as I loved writing it. I hope it gave you a chance to escape the real world for a little while. Thanks for giving me a chance to become one of your favorite authors. See you in the next book.

Wishing you all peace, love, and happiness,
Morgan

About the Author

Morgan Beacham lives in a small coastal town with her husband, who is a Firefighter/EMT, and two children. When Morgan is not putting out metaphorical fires at home, she is immersed in nature, reading, writing, and all things romance.

She is a teacher-turned-author who also provides editing and proofreading services, since even authors need to eat. In the little bit of spare time she can find, Morgan volunteers for animal nonprofits and literature-centric organizations because animals and books need someone to speak for them, too.

Let's keep in touch!
Facebook: Morgan Beacham Author
Instagram: Morgan Beacham Author
Goodreads: Morgan Beacham
Bookbub: Morganbeachamauthor
www.morganbeacham.com